Metaphorosis

October 2023

Beautifully made speculative fiction

Also from Metaphorosis

Metaphorosis Magazine

Metaphorosis: Best of 20xx
Metaphorosis 20xx: The Complete Stories
annual issues, from 2016
Monthly issues

Plant Based Press

Best Vegan Science Fiction & Fantasy
annual issues, 2016-2020

from B. Morris Allen:
Chambers of the Heart: speculative stories
Susurrus
Allenthology: Volume I
Tocsin: and other stories
Start with Stones: collected stories
Metaphorosis: a collection of stories

Verdage

Reading 5X5 x3: Changes
Reading 5X5 x2: Duets
Score: an SFF symphony
Reading 5X5: Readers' Edition
Reading 5X5: Writers' Edition

Vestige

The Nocturnals, by Mariah Montoya

Joyful Heave

Museum Piece: an unusual collection

Metaphorosis

October 2023

edited by
B. Morris Allen

ISSN: 2573-136X (online)
ISBN: 978-1-64076-267-1 (e-book)
ISBN: 978-1-64076-268-8 (paperback)

Metaphorosis
a magazine of speculative fiction
from
Metaphorosis Publishing

Neskowin

October 2023

Any Day Now

K. E. Redmond

She pushed the intercom button and waited, taking in the sprawling brick pile that was the Unadilla Senior Living Community. It could have passed for a grand manor or a country club, but the ramps at the doors were a dead give-away, even if she hadn't seen one or two geriatrics, bundled to the eyes, cruising the grounds with their walkers. She wondered where they were going. There wasn't anything around for miles.

She'd driven out from Boston, taking the Interstate west, then backroads where despite GPS, Unadilla's entrance eluded her. Finally, she found it, nearly hidden in the undergrowth; two stone pillars with a non-descript sign and a chain link fence stretching off through the woods on both sides. The razor wire was unexpected, though, and driving up to the main building she noticed discreet security cameras at intervals. Somehow, she wasn't surprised when hers was the only car in the lot. Walking to the front door, she looked to the north where the sky looked threatening. It still hadn't snowed this winter; it was certainly cold enough. But any day. She hoped it would hold off until she got home. She hated driving in the snow.

The intercom crackled. "May I help you?"

"Yes. I'm here to see Professor Cervine. Professor John Cervine. He's expecting me." The first lie. A small one. His reply to her email requesting an interview had been more of an open ended, 'We'll see'.

"Your name?"

"Kat. Kat Dobrovolsky. But he called me Dobs. I mean, that's how he'll remember me."

"One moment."

Behind the glass-paneled door, a shadow crossed the room.

Kat recalled another time she'd waited to see the Professor, outside another door. It had been the beginning of her sophomore year, outside his department office. Through the frosted sidelight, she had been able to make out two shadows inside. One of them she knew was Trey Tottenger, the only sophomore to ever make the varsity team, he of the blinding smile and chiseled torso, catnip to cheerleaders everywhere. She'd met him once at a freshman mixer. He'd draped an arm around her and told her she had nice eyes. She reasoned, accurately enough, that he was both drunk and competing in the ancient and fraternal sport of bagging the homeliest frosh. She was reluctantly prying him off when he spied a more viable target and staggered away. Anyway, outside the Professor's office, he'd walked by like she didn't exist.

"No exceptions," the woman on the Registrar Desk had told her. "The Professor interviews all students for his Astronomy 101 course. Don't worry," she said with a grimace. "He'll be quick. Good luck."

So she sat, listening to the low murmur of voices inside the office, although the conversation sounded one-sided.

Abruptly, the door swung open, and Trey Tottenger stomped out, red to his ears. A voice called after him, "I'd recommend basket weaving. You'd at least graduate with a skill." A pause. "Next!"

Kat sidled in. The only chair was positioned directly across the desk from the Professor. He was older than she'd expected, snow white hair in waves to his shirt collar, the hand that waved her in flecked with liver spots. But his eyes, when he looked up, were blue, bright, oddly intense.

"Major?" he barked as she slid into the chair.

"Uh, English."

"I see." He rapped the desktop with his pencil. "Let me guess. You needed a science credit and decided my course wouldn't be too much of a heavy lift."

She nodded, then quickly shook her head.

"Well, which is it?" he snapped. "Yes or no?"

She felt a hot flush rise. He was trying to fluster her; that pissed her off. "Yes, I need a science credit. But I really want to know more about the universe."

"Is that so you can write odes to the summer's full moon?" He waved his hand languidly. *'Art thou pale for weariness, of climbing heaven and gazing on the earth, wandering companionless, among the stars that have a different birth.'* He snorted. "You're wasting your time. Wordsworth did it better than you could ever hope."

"Shelley." Kat returned his stare with a bland look. "That's Shelley. Not Wordsworth."

The Professor grinned. "Speak truth to power, my dear. I stand corrected. Alright, for entry to my class and all the marbles, tell me what you think is the most significant advance humankind has made in space exploration in the last one-hundred years." He leaned back, closing his eyes, lacing his fingers across his paunch. "I'll warn you," he murmured, "your predecessor in that chair thought it might be warp drive. I hope you can do better."

Kat thought for a moment. "Voyager," she said finally.

He sounded bored. "I imagine you're referring to the television series. Or, lord help me, to that benighted movie with the aliens who couldn't spell? Vegan? Verger?"

"V-ger. No. The Voyager space probes."

He opened his eyes; she thought he almost looked surprised. "Explain."

"Because when we launched the probes we looked outward, not in. We said, hello, is anyone out there? We didn't just look up and wonder. We took the leap. We hoped." She stopped, embarrassed.

The Professor closed his eyes again. "Acceptable. Pick up your books in the bookstore. There will be two papers and a final. Do not be late for class. Next!"

A buzz, a click, and she was back waiting in the cold. The door opened. A muscular man in scrubs and a high fade stood inside the entry, a small bare foyer behind him. She noticed there was no reception desk, no chairs. They really didn't get many visitors. He motioned her in.

"Miss Dobrovolsky? I'm Frank, Professor Cervine's health care aide." He looked her over. "The Professor didn't say anyone was coming today. Is he expecting you?"

She gave him her most engaging smile. "He said come anytime, so here I am. I hope that's okay. It was kind of a long drive."

"Oh? Where are you coming from?"

"Boston. I was back in the area visiting and thought I'd drive over to see my old professor. I was a huge fan. Well, me and about a thousand other students. He's—was—just an incredible lecturer. Getting into one of his courses was cutthroat. I did his introductory course, and I was hooked. Not that I went into the sciences. No brain for numbers. But I've always loved astronomy. And he was one of my advisors on my senior thesis. Sorry," she stopped, blushing. "I'm babbling." Lie number two, well-buried. But it had done the trick. Frank's wary look faded to polite boredom.

"That's okay. He's feeling pretty good today, so you're in luck. Follow me, I'll take you to him." They headed down a long brightly lit corridor with tasteful bucolic reproductions on soothing pastel walls. At regular intervals on both sides, they passed numbered doors. At her Nana's facility, all the residents decorated the doors to their rooms. Photos of grandkids. Artwork. Political signs. Holiday wreaths. Not here. One door was like the next. Uniform. Regimented. Frank stopped outside Room A219, his hand on the knob. "What was your thesis on, if you don't mind me asking?"

"Uhm. Cultural acceptance and acclimation to scientific progression through mass media saturation. Yeah, it's a mouthful. I was an English major."

"The elevator version?"

"Basically, figuring out how often people need to read or hear about some scientific breakthrough before they actually believe it."

"And did you? Figure it out?"

"Not really. People are hard. They believe stupid things all the time for their own reasons. And once they do, it's hard to shift them."

"Everyone thinks they've got the inside track, huh?"

"That's right."

He didn't move to open the door. "So, you're a journalist?"

Her smile tightened. "Not quite. Science writer, slash editor. I translate what the science guys write into something actual people can understand. Those who can't do, write, I guess."

"Working on anything now?"

There was no point trying to get by him, she had to play. Lie number three coming up.

"A children's book. Introduction to the giants of astronomy. You know, Newton, Copernicus, Galileo."

"Professor Cervine?"

She shook her head. "He's big, but not quite in their league. I was hoping to run the list by him though, see if I missed anyone. And catch up on how he's doing, of course." Lie number four.

He took the hint. "Right. He tires easily, so I'll ask you to keep your visit short." He opened the door and stuck his head in. "Professor? Your guest is here. I'll be down the hall if you need me." He stood aside to let her in. She could feel Frank's eyes on her back for a long moment. Then, quietly, the door closed behind her.

The room was like any university professor's office: crammed bookcases, drifts of paper, professional journals stacked in corners, and a desk barely visible beneath the detritus. All typical, apart from the hospital bed near the window. Its occupant turned his head on the pillow to regard her, his eyes overlarge in a skull pared down to a few strands of white hair and skin thin as tissue paper, sallow, and wrinkled.

"Professor Cervine? Remember me? Kathy Dobrovolsky."

He raised a bony hand from the crisp white sheets, immediately dropped it, as though the effort was exhausting.

"Well, come in. Don't stand there gawking. Find your seat. I can't stand late arrivals. Disrupts my chain of thought. Disrupts the class. Hurry up." The tone was testy, but the voice was nearly as she remembered, giving the lie to the frail form.

She scurried over to the chair beside the bed, throwing her coat across the back, and sat down, setting her handbag at her feet. He stared hard at her. She stared back.

"Do I know you?"

"Yes, Professor. We spoke. Well, we texted. I was one of your students at university. You knew me as Kathy Dobs. Well, that's what you called me. I've come to say hello."

"Have you?" He looked away. She followed his gaze. Outside the windows, an aide pushed a wheelchair containing an elderly man bent nearly double in the seat. "I don't do outings, if that's what you had in mind."

"We don't need to, if you don't want. I brought you the last print copy of the

British Astrophysics Journal. I thought you'd like it."

He turned back, looking peeved. "The last?"

She shrugged apologetically. "They're going online. Save the trees."

He made a noise between a snarl and a sneeze. "Continuous publication since the 1800s and now it's some mishmash on a computer screen. What depths will we plumb next? Lego models of the universe? Well? Give it to me."

She handed it over. "I was in Oxford looking at Sir Isaac Newton's papers. I was writing a piece for a magazine there. The editor said he knew you. I think he was one of your graduate students."

Frankly, she'd been surprised by the assignment. Out of the blue, the magazine had reached out to her, all expenses paid to the U.K., top dollar for an article any hack could have written. Who did that?

The Professor flipped open to the table of contents, running a finger down the titles. "I can't be expected to remember the names of all my students. And Newton was at Cambridge. Wrong place entirely."

"Yes, I know. But the Bodleian had a recent acquisition from a private library.

An amateur astronomer. Contemporary of Newton's."

"May is still banging on about cosmic dust, I see," he grumbled, flicking the journal page with a finger that looked too fragile to take that kind of abuse. "I told him to move on, but he never listens. It's dirt! Get over it. What were you saying about Newton?"

"One of his contemporaries. It turns out, they exchanged several letters. That's what I was looking at in the Bodleian."

He flung the journal down on the bed and fixed her with a glare perfected during eons of oral exams and faculty meetings.

"In my experience, correspondence between such intellectually mismatched individuals as Sir Isaac Newton and some dilettante in knee pants is useful only as mulch. I see you hesitate. Let me guess, this unknown pen pal told our boy Newton he'd transmuted lead into gold."

She smiled. "There was some of that."

"Why am I not surprised."

"Not all of it. One of Newton's letters was interesting."

"Was it? You sound pleased with yourself." He scowled at her. "Don't be coy. It's boring."

"Newton wrote to this friend about an astronomical observation he'd made. He described it as, 'A most wonderous sight. Three nights standing.' Based on his notes, he was describing something near or possibly from the star Elnath, in the Taurus Constellation."

"I hadn't realized our English department was churning out qualified astronomers these days. Elnath? That's 100 light years away."

"131. He reported it in 1700."

"I know when Sir Isaac lived," he retorted. "I'm not senile. Yet." His fingers beat a tattoo on the sheet. "And so?"

"So?" she repeated blankly.

He clicked his tongue against his front teeth impatiently. "Does this particle, this mere mote of information carry some earth-shaking import? Elnath, as far as I am aware, would not be described as a wonderous sight. Giant star. Blue-white in color. Nothing to write home about, so to speak."

"True, but it made me curious. What did he see exactly? Who else saw it?" This part always excited her. She couldn't help it. "So, I started digging. Did you know that one hundred years before Newton, Copernicus studied the occultation of

Aldebaran? Also, in the Taurus Constellation."

"Oooooh, I'm getting goose bumps. Two astronomers studied stars in the same constellation. Rewrite the textbooks!" He rolled his eyes.

She fished in her handbag, pulled out her phone, holding the screen up for him to see. "I found a note he made, marginalia, about the star Alcyone. He wrote, and I quote, *'Trinitas in tenebris. Mirabilis.'* 'Trinity from the darkness. Wonderous.' Trinity. Three. Just like Newton's three nights. And wonderous. Obviously, they saw something similar."

He sighed. "No, obviously you are in thrall to an illusion peculiar to our ignorant times, my dear. That there must be a causal connection between two completely unrelated events."

She ignored him. "I kept digging. I went back in history to observations by Chinese astronomers. Year 1054, the supernova in the Crab Nebula. Incidentally, also in Taurus."

"Let me guess," he sighed. "Three sightings or events or however you're mislabeling them."

She ignored that too. "I couldn't believe it. Three unique observations that can be traced back to some part of the Taurus Constellation. Professor," she leaned in, lowering her voice. "I think there's a pattern. I think this is contact."

He snorted. "Contact? I presume you mean some alien intelligence signaling to us from across the universe. Based on what? Three random observations? Do you have any concept of the distances you're describing? How vast? No. You were probably watching cat videos on your little phone when I covered that topic in class. I'll put it in terms you might understand. One light year is 5.88 trillion miles. Rounding up so even you may comprehend, six trillion is 6 with 12 zeros behind it. Alcyone is 370 light years away, the Crab Nebula is, let me see," he paused, but only for a second, "6,523 light years away. Multiply either number by a 6 with all those little zeroes and you'll realize you're talking complete nonsense."

She edged her chair closer to the bed. "But Professor, I've found others."

"Paleolithic cave drawings?" he scoffed. "Some daubing of stars on rocks."

"What about the WOW signal? August 15, 1977. A signal was detected by Ohio State University's Big Ear radio telescope for 72 seconds. It came from the Sagittarius constellation."

"Discredited. Never detected again. Or do you imagine your aliens are playing some intergalactic game of ring the doorbell and run away? Besides, you're mixing your constellations. Or are you simply throwing anything into the pot to prove your point?"

She sat back, silent.

"Have I stymied you?" he sneered. "Good. Next time, get your facts straight before you bother me with nonsense." He shifted in bed, closing his eyes. "I think I've had enough entertainment for today. Go away."

"Humor me. One more."

He opened his eyes to object but saw the mulish look on her face. "In 1945," she began, "a graduate student at our old university—who will remain nameless—observed a signal originating from Alpha Tauri, 65 light years away."

"Odd, I've never seen anything published. That would have been quite the coup," he said.

"It was rumored the War Department suppressed his paper in the interests of national security. They probably thought they had enough problems with a world war here on earth without worrying about extraterrestrials."

"You're citing rumors now! The true hallmark of a failed argument," he said. The contempt in his voice stung her.

"He was—is—a dedicated and brilliant astronomer. He believed in rigorous scientific observation."

"Sounds like a swot. Did your Bodleian friends tell you what a swot is?" he asked sweetly.

She leaned in, lowering her voice. "Also, he was a little anal about keeping stuff. I know, because I helped him pack it up. Books, notes, drafts. He squirreled everything away. In time, I imagine, he completely forgot he'd kept a draft. It happens. A lifetime of stuff piles up, retirement rolls around. Who wants to go through all that paper? Just box it up and shove it into the archives. Forget it. Practical obscurity."

The door opened. Frank stuck his head in. "You ready, Professor?"

Cervine who had been lying in bed, immobile, nearly levitated. "Get out! I'll tell you when I'm ready. Get! Out!"

Frank's head disappeared; Kathy sat back.

"Oh, don't look so worried," the Professor growled. "I haven't thrown you out. Yet." But the outburst seemed to have drained him. He lay back against his pillows, his breathing labored. He took a deep breath.

"This feels like explaining fission to a sleep-deprived toddler, but let me try," he said. "In terms of the Earth's development, all 4.5 billion years of it, our pathetic human civilization is but a blip. Less than the last half-second on the timeline. For an exceedingly small portion of that time, barely 60 years, we have actively looked for others of our kind, although I am at a loss to understand why. We don't get along with the neighbors we have. Regardless, we've listened for signs of intelligent life in the universe. And do you know what we've heard?"

"But..."

He held up a hand, forestalling her. "Nothing. We've heard nothing. Of course, techno transmissions may be exceedingly rare. Maybe none have crossed our path in the last 60 years. Maybe they only transmit to our part of the universe every 100 years or so." He chuckled. "The other equally valid possibility is there are no transmissions to receive."

"Carl Sagan said..." Kathy interrupted.

He groaned. "Dear Carl. Let me guess: 'The universe is a pretty big place. If it's just us, seems like an awful waste of space.' Spare me."

"We're finding earth-like planets every day. Based on dozens of factors, one researcher estimated an intelligent civilization would be at most 17,000 light years away. And that was in a peer-reviewed publication," she added quickly.

"Pie-eyed optimists. And how do you suggest we talk with them? We have no technology that can transmit to those distances. And what would be the point? Our message, optimally sent at the speed of light, reaches them; they send one back. Do you really believe there will be anyone here to receive it? As a species, we'll be lucky to survive into the next century."

"But that's my point, Professor. They're not sending a message. They're coming here. Look at it: Crab Nebula, 6,523 light years away; Alcyone, 370 light years; Elnath, 131; Alpha Tauri, 65 light years. Every time, they're getting closer."

"Please listen to the voice of reason. I'm sure I covered this in one of my lectures, it was certainly an exam question. The Space Shuttle travels five miles a second. At that speed, optimistically, how long would it take a person—or an E.T., if you insist—to travel one light year?"

"37,200 years," she replied. "I got it right on the exam."

"I'm sure you did. And yet, you believe these intergalactic interlopers, these E.T.s, are traveling hundreds of light years within the span of our own written history. It is not possible. Do the math. It should be well within even your limited capabilities."

"But suppose they can travel faster than light?"

"Impossible!"

"They said men flying and the Higgs boson particle were impossible, too. How else would you explain the signals? They're leap-frogging across the universe."

"I've always envied the latitude writers have to wax poetic when they fail to understand basic science," he murmured. "I sincerely hope you're not thinking of writing about this wild theory of yours. You'll be finished, professionally. Unless you enjoy being lumped in with the crazies and conspiracy nuts."

He waggled a hand in the direction of the carafe on his nightstand. She jumped up to pour him a glass of water, waiting while he took a sip. As he handed the glass back, he held her gaze.

"Do you remember what I wrote on your thesis?" he asked. She looked blank for a moment, then her eyes widened. "I see you do. You always were a bright one. My final affirmation of all your hard work. Do not disappoint me now." He slid down in bed. "Trying to reason with you has been exhausting. Thank you for coming. Leave."

Frank was waiting for her in the hallway. "Good visit?"

She nodded. "So-so. I think I upset him."

"Believe it or not, he was in a good mood today. Get everything you need?"

"What?" She wished Frank would shut up so she could think. Her thesis, where had she packed it?

"Did you talk to him about the book?" He stopped beside the front entrance, watching her. "You said you needed to talk to him about your children's book."

"Oh. No. We got off on a tangent. That's okay."

"Yeah? Say, about your thesis. You said the Professor was one of your advisors. I'll bet he had some good comments. He always has a lot to say."

"You know him," she replied, going over in her head the boxes she'd stored in the attic at her parent's house. There wasn't much room in a studio apartment. The thesis had to be in there somewhere.

"So, like what?" He was waiting, all friendly curiosity. But his persistence made her wary.

"I'm not sure," she said slowly. "Something about science needing more scribes." Lie number five. She was getting good at this.

"That's harsh." He opened the door. "Have a safe trip back. Looks like the snow's holding off. But any day now, it's going to get here."

She nodded. It wasn't until she was back on the Interstate that she thought about Frank's questions. How had he known the Professor had asked about her thesis? She checked the rear-view mirror and sped up.

In his bed, the Professor waited. He could practically predict the next move. So when the phone on his bedside table rang, he let it ring itself out. In the quiet, he felt the sweet pull of sleep. The phone rang again, jarring him awake. This time he picked up.

"I'm sleeping," he snapped, then listened in silence. "No, I don't see any need for concern. A tissue of conjecture and twaddle. Yes, I told her that," he replied. "I have no idea if she'll listen to her favorite professor, as you so unctuously phrase it. I can tell you she's bluffing about my papers. I went through them all myself. As I'm sure you did." He listened again with a bored look. "Your threats are wasted on me. You harbor the mistaken belief I care what you do to me now. And tell that useless blob you call my aide not to disturb me." He hung up. The phone remained resolutely mute. Still, for a long time he kept watch on the driveway, alert for comings and goings. After a while, darkness obscured the distant tree line, then gathered itself up to fill the room. The stars appeared. Tomorrow maybe there'd be snow, but tonight the sky was clear and cold.

He looked up at the twinkling lights, seeking out the constellation Taurus, the bull. Catalogued by Ptolemy in the second century, known since the Bronze Age. In the Northern Hemisphere, the constellation passes through the sky from November to March but is most visible in January. That was a lift from one of his lectures. What had she called it? Leap frogging. Inelegant, but accurate. He preferred a skipping stone. The Crab Nebula, Alcyone, Elnath, Alpha Tauri. Closer and closer. And the last one, from his red dwarf, 8.72 light years away, the signal he'd detected when he'd nearly given up hope, just before his abrupt and unwilling retirement. In terms of the universe, 8.72 light years was practically next door. He hadn't bothered trying to publish this time. He was too old and tired to fight them now, but he wasn't going to let the knowledge die with him. When she'd asked him to be her senior thesis advisor, he'd agreed, already plotting. If the universe teaches you one thing, it is the long view. Signing off on her thesis, he'd written the signal coordinates for the red dwarf as though they were random scribbles. His way of telling her, when she finally put it all together, that she was right.

He'd counted on them discounting her. Wrong major. Wrong sex. Why did they always underestimate women? But she was bright, and she'd always been stubborn. He'd known she'd figure it out eventually. With his help, of course. All the breadcrumbs he'd strewn in her path. The draft of his so-long ago graduate paper, his notes on the red dwarf, left where she had to find them, packing up his office. The magazine assignment he'd finagled for her. Little nudges. Trusting to her curiosity to piece it all together. And with the internet, social media, she had resources he'd never dreamed of. This time they'd have trouble stuffing that genie back in the bottle. Let them try. Speak truth to power, indeed.

He recited it over and over like a mantra. Crab, Alcyone, Elnath, Alpha Tauri, 6,523, 370, 131, 65, 8.72 light years away. Getting closer. He almost wished he'd be around for it. In the dark, he chuckled. They'd run in circles screaming. He could just hear them. The stock market would have a seizure, if it didn't crash. The arrival of extraterrestrials would certainly take the shine off capitalism. Not to mention organized religion. Where do little green men fit in God's great plan? Do they get their own image of the Deity, their own

Savior? Their own heaven? It would almost be worth it to hear how they worked aliens into Creation. Countdown: 6,523, 370, 131, 65, 8.72.

He smiled slyly at Taurus. "Any day now. Any day."

*See K.E. Redmond's story "Any Day Now"
online at Metaphorosis.
If you liked it, leave a comment. Authors love
that!
Remember to subscribe to our e-mail updates so
you'll know when new stories are posted.*

About the story

The idea for this story came while I was reading about the search for life on other planets for a course on the mysteries of the cosmos. It struck me that alien life is not as improbable as it might seem. In fact, it's downright probable. Of course, then I wondered what the official reaction might be here on Earth to signs of intelligent life. "Any Day Now" was the result.

A question for the author

Q: Do you make art other than prose? What kind, and how is it different?

A: Do I make art other than prose? Isn't that hard enough? But yes, I paint and sculpt, in addition to my writing. My painting is old school representational. I like the effort it takes to really see something as it is. On the other hand, my sculptures tend to be fantastic. I identify with that mythology of creators breathing life into their creations. It's just something about the malleability of clay.

About the author

K.E. Redmond writes about the extraordinary possibilities of our everyday world, that interstice shared by mystery and hard science.

Salaatu

Lisa Short

After two days of the carriage's relentless jolting, Darya felt battered to the point of numbness. She fixed her own eyes on her hands, clenched tightly together on her lap—she still wore her librarian's smock and kirtle, ruched at the neck and laced down the sides, the fabric bunching up under her curled fingers. That lacing seemed to tighten up hourly, and the fleeting handful of stops over the past two days had not included time to bathe or change. She itched now, miserably, and surreptitious squirming did nothing to ease it.

Outside the carriage door's single small window, the sparse pine forest that dotted the flat, still winter-brown landscape jolted past, nothing like the rich glory of trees that grew in the foothills of the Imperial capital. But this landscape *was* familiar, drearily so—though Darya had not returned home since her grandfather had won her the appointment to the Imperial Library five years before. The school had been grueling, the few holidays granted librarial students mostly given to sleeping off the exhaustion of constant work-study. And after graduation, her place in the Library had been so new, she hadn't wanted to seem less dedicated, less *aspiring*, than any of the other newly minted underlibrarians—

—and, all other variously true excuses aside, she hadn't wanted to go back home. She *had* missed her grandfather, the measure of her love for him increasing nearly every day she had been away, discovering anew every hour what joy she found in the sheer volume of scholarship and knowledge suddenly available to her in overflowing measure. She *had* missed him, and would have loved nothing more than to speak to him of her studies, of all the Library's books and maps and registries, a love she knew well he shared.

But she hadn't missed the rest of her family, and she hadn't missed her home village of Korshun. She *certainly* hadn't missed the seashore, nor the sea, nor anything living *in* or *on* it—and perhaps, if she insisted on it long enough, it might even become the truth. Darya jerked her gaze away from the window and back down to her white-knuckled fists once more.

The driver's muffled shout was barely enough warning for Darya to grab for the bar beside her head; the carriage jounced and shuddered to a halt. Seconds later a guard, large and expressionless, pulled the door open and held out his hand to her. She blinked down at it in surprise; he took her hesitation for reluctance and caught her wrist up in one rough hand, pulling her up from the seat and out the door.

The other carriage, in spite of its greater size, had beaten them to this chosen campsite—its outriders already had a bonfire built. The fire dazzled Darya's eyes; she looked away, blinking, and her gaze fell upon two men standing some distance back from the fire, deep in conversation. The taller of the two looked up, and Darya had a moment of mere cataloging without identification—silver hair, cut like a soldier's, long thin face, narrow lips—then those lips turned up at the corners, and the shock of recognition drove the blood from her head in a rush.

She hurried forward and dropped into deep curtsey, a prelude to full genuflection, but he shook his head briefly at her as she bent lower still. "There's no need for that here, *Maya* Darya." Was it only the firelight that made the lines carved deeply around his eyes and mouth sharper than they had been just a few days before? "My physician"—a nod in the other, younger man's direction —"insisted we stop for the night." Darya tore her gaze from the Emperor's drawn features to his companion's, startled to find he was already staring at her—*glaring* at her. She recoiled involuntarily, a movement she tried hard to disguise as a shiver in the chill night air. The Emperor followed her gaze; his mouth compressed in fleeting annoyance. "Do be courteous to our guest. If nothing else, she is expanding our knowledge of the natural history of our own lands. I would have thought you'd be pleased by that, at least."

"Sire, this isn't knowledge, it's *mythology*. These sea demons—" Darya bit back a hiss of protest, clenching her jaw to remain silent. "—or whatever they are, if they even exist—Sire, your own reforms, the medical colleges you created in the first years of your reign, a half-century ago! were designed to eliminate the charlatanry and yes, *dangerous* ignorance of these backwater beliefs—"

"The *salaatu* aren't myths," said the Emperor, mildly, though his gaze had narrowed on the young man's half-averted face. "The *maya* could doubtless show you where in the Imperial Library to find the many historical references—documented evidence—of their existence." His annoyance softened into obvious affection. "Truly, Aison. My father had some dealings with these sea people—*not* demons—in his oceangoing days, before he was designated my great-uncle's heir."

So the young man was Aison—*Loro* Aison, a fourth- or fifth-degree relation of the Emperor himself and, she'd heard gossiped more than once, fanatically devoted to him. Then the Emperor waved her away, not unkindly; she obediently hurried backwards, once more out of earshot, though judging from Aison's passionate expression the argument still continued. One of the servants scurrying past thrust a bundle into Darya's arms; shaking it out, she found herself in possession of a roll of thick quilts. A quick glance around confirmed that several of the guards were clambering awkwardly into their own, not even removing mail shirts or boots. The outriders were erecting a tent, for the Emperor and likely *Loro* Aison, Darya supposed. Well, the air didn't smell like rain was imminent, and anything was better than sleeping sitting up in miserable snatches in the carriage. She shook her bedroll out too and after some experimentation, managed to squeeze most of herself inside it.

The brackish, muggy edge to the breeze, carried westward from the still-unseen ocean, pricked at her even as exhaustion pulled her down into the oblivion of sleep. The shadows behind her closed eyelids gradually morphed into dreams of the sea, obsidian swells limned with phosphorescence under a pallid moon.

Darya had been seven years old the summer the *salaatu* had come to Korshun. She'd been playing near the shore, hot and listless; she had heard them before she'd seen them, a singing like the ocean wind blowing over the shells the queen conches left scattered along the shoreline. She'd squinted up at the horizon, seen something dark bobbing upon the waves in the distance, not quite the right shape to be one of the village fishing boats.

The singing had grown louder, oddly compelling—then, between one blink of her eyes and the next, the shadow on the horizon had materialized into a long boat larger even than the village headman's, the biggest in the fleet. A tent was been lashed to its deck; as Darya gaped at it, an enormous woman wearing nothing but a headdress of coral-studded feathers strolled leisurely out onto the bow.

"Ha!"

The cry, shockingly close, had startled Darya into stumbling backwards, her foot coming down hard on a rock, her ankle twisting painfully. Rough warm fingers had clamped around her wrist as she fell sideways with a cry of her own.

Yanked neatly back onto her feet by those same fingers, Darya had found herself staring up at a stranger's distressed face. That in of itself had been an astonishment—no strangers had ever come to Korshun in her short lifetime. This one, perhaps a few years older than Darya, was barefoot and barelegged, her shirt a mere strip of cloth tied around her narrow chest.

"Are you all right?" She'd spoken strangely—Darya had never met anyone for whom Imperial Oun was not their first language, and the musical rippling of the girl's speech fascinated her. Then the girl looked down at Darya's dress, her heavy dark brows drawing so far down they nearly met over her nose. "Why are you wearing so many clothes? Are you cold?"

The girl's name, Darya discovered, was Sayu—nothing like any name Darya had ever heard, as Sayu herself was nothing like anyone she'd ever met. And the rest of that summer, for the first time in her life, Darya had been grateful for how little attention her family paid her. They cared nothing if she disappeared for hours, as long as she was back in the manor by supper.

"But you can't swim?" Sayu had asked in astonishment, the third morning they'd met at the shore's edge. "*Babies* can swim! Perhaps you've just forgotten how?" Assured that was not the case, she'd sputtered, "But what have you been doing instead?"

Not knowing what else to say, Darya had muttered something about liking to read. "Read?" Sayu's lips had pursed as she'd rolled the word over her tongue. "*Read.* It sounds ugly. Does it hurt?"

It had been Darya's turn to laugh and then explain, though Sayu's puzzlement hadn't seemed much eased. "Oh? Well, it sounds lonely. Swimming's far more fun. I'll teach you!" She'd looked enormously pleased by the idea.

The *salaatu* had sailed up and down Oun's northeastern coast on their own inscrutable business, frequently returning to Korshun for a few days' or a week's rest —and whenever Darya sighted their boat, bobbing gently against its beachrock moorings, she ran as fast as she could to the shore, likelier than not to find Sayu already there and waiting for her. But finally, the day after the autumn equinox, Sayu had clasped Darya's hands tightly enough to hurt and had said abruptly, "I have to go."

Darya hadn't protested, but she hadn't been able to stop the tears that had welled up either. She'd opened her mouth, meaning to say something stoic and brave, and had sobbed aloud instead. Sayu had pulled her close, resting her cheek against the top of Darya's head, and they had stood like that until her sobs had ceased. "But we'll be back," Sayu had said, her voice muffled against Darya's hair. "Next summer. I promise—"

Darya awoke to something poking her shoulder. She pried her eyes open, squinting in the dull gray light of dawn, to the unwelcome sight of a guard crouching over her. "We're leaving," he said flatly, and withdrew as soon as it was clear she'd understood him.

The sparse scatter of trees outside were thickening, the ragged evergreens now interspersed with fatter, paler trunks, lightly dusted with the first leaves of early spring. *Home...Grandfather.* She had treasured, still treasured, his handful of letters to her over the years, his obvious pride in her accomplishments in the Imperial capital—she flinched a little at the thought of those letters, abandoned and unsecured in her small clothespress in the underlibrarians' dormitory. Losing them would be a blow; hopefully nobody would find them interesting enough to steal.

The winter after the *salaatu* first sailed away, Darya had crept into the manor library, determined to assuage her now-unbearable loneliness by finding out more about the *salaatu* themselves. Her grandfather had happened upon her there one evening, her nose buried deep in an encyclopedia. She'd been too young to understand then how the rest of the family had feared his scholarly and acerbic wit—to eight-year-old Darya he'd been no more fearsome than any other member of the household, all seemingly alike in their disdain for her existence.

She understood far better now, his awkward and stilted enthusiasm at the sight of anybody other than himself voluntarily opening a book. She'd told him willingly enough of her curiosity about the *salaatu*, and had shown him what little she'd found about them in the library.

"But I'm sure they aren't *sea demons*, Grandfather—"

"Indeed not," her grandfather had agreed with some indignation, and bent down over the open encyclopedia far enough that his nose nearly touched the pages. "Let me see that—

hmph!" He straightened back up, flipping the pages rapidly backwards until he reached the very front. "I should have known. Sornois wrote this. Incompetent *and* a coward." Darya had blinked up at him warily—he hadn't appeared angry at *her*, at least, though she had no idea who Sornois was. "Likely he was writing it to pacify the then-emperor—this edition is over a century old." Her grandfather abruptly clapped the book shut, causing a small geyser of dust to erupt from its binding, then gazed narrowly down at Darya. "I'm delighted to see that you aren't credulous enough to believe everything you read." He paused. "And that you chose to try to find the answer to a question about the natural world in a book."

He'd seemed to be waiting for a reply, so Darya had gathered up her courage and ventured, "I, I *do* like books, Grandfather. But—" she did her best to ignore the beginnings of the lowering frown on his brow, because she really did want to know, "—how do you know which books to believe, and which not? If you want to know something?"

His eyebrows lifted, erasing the frown lines as if by magic; Darya, who had been quailing inside—questions were generally not encouraged, at least not her questions and not those put to an adult of the household—was heartened by the sudden gleam of warmth in his dark eyes. "Now *that* is a question of worth, Granddaughter." She started a little; it was almost as if he'd seen what she was thinking. "And it's a very important one. Come, let me show you something."

He had gone on to show Darya a great many things—not only the marvelous stories hidden in his books, but the science of the books themselves—how they came to be written, how to understand the meaning beneath the obvious words, how to search for additional books to verify (or refute) the contents of any other. Her grandfather's library, it had turned out, was as full of joyous surprises as the summer had been with Sayu.

Darya's first sight of the village outskirts now, through the carriage window, made her stomach clench tight. Even the meanest shack had at least one guard stationed at its door— unable to help herself, she glanced up at the manor house looming silently atop its hill. Guards manned both front doors, and likely were standing at the postern gate as well. Her gaze darted to the grounds—yes, she could still see the faint, blackened remains of the old stillroom. Her grandfather had refused to rebuild it there, had insisted on moving the new stillroom to its own building, completely out of sight of the manor. She had heard him shouting at her mother one night as she lay sleepless in her bed, wracked with the pain of her burns—her grandfather, who had never before raised his voice in her hearing—

But there was no reason to suppose that all the manor's inhabitants weren't perfectly all right. She understood why the Emperor would want to keep his presence, and especially his purpose, an absolute secret. The fact that he was taking such pains to keep everyone ignorant of what might be happening outside their homes was evidence enough that he intended them no harm in the long run.

Once again, the Emperor's carriage had outpaced hers; after they'd jolted to a halt, the stone-faced guard from the day before escorted her straight to the Emperor's tent. Once inside, Darya curtseyed, darting lightning-fast glances at the Emperor's face to gauge whether he wanted her to skip full genuflection once more. It was still rather unreal, to be standing nearly within touching distance of him—close enough that the scent of his cologne tickled her nose, to see the shadows like bruises etched deep beneath those ostensibly friendly eyes.

"So, *maya.* How do we contact the *salaatu?*"

Darya took a deep, fortifying breath. "We don't. Not from the shore." She had tried to explain that before, back at the palace. "They came themselves, in the summer, in their own boats. We never summoned them."

The warmth in his eyes dimmed. "Then how do you propose to bring them here?"

Darya's frantic, scurrying thoughts during that first sleepless night in the carriage had finally settled on a possibility. "There is a place I used to go with," she took another deep breath, "one of them sometimes. A few leagues out to sea. When we were children." And a bit older, too, but there was really no need to elaborate on that. "I can swim out to it. It's in their territory; they may realize someone is there, even if they aren't sure who it is. They're likely to investigate." *Eventually.* Well, it was the best idea she'd been able to come up with.

"Swim out to it? By yourself?" The Emperor's face had gone very still; his lips barely moved as he spoke. "Why don't we take the village boats to it? *All* of us?"

Darya flinched. "It's underwater. A fair bit underwater. Even if any of your guards or servants—or yourself, or *Loro* Aison—are unusually strong swimmers, you probably wouldn't be able to follow me there." It was hard to force out the next words. "I...have some ability to swim the way the *salaatu* do." Her fists clenched, hidden deep in her skirts. "I did tell you, Sire, that you might not want the healing —it doesn't leave you unchanged, from what you were before."

The Emperor's dark blue gaze shifted from her face to a point beyond her right shoulder. "Aison. The *maya* says she must swim out to sea, underwater and alone." He smiled, thinly—his smile at her the night before had indeed held genuine warmth, because by contrast this one held none at all. "I recall that you did some sailing as a boy, with your father— why don't you take her out that few leagues, so she doesn't dangerously tire herself reaching this meeting place?"

"Certainly, Sire," came *Loro* Aison's voice, behind her—she hadn't even heard him enter the tent. She curtseyed deeply once more and followed Aison back outside.

Aison had commandeered someone's yoal. He handled it, and its simple square sail, well enough, which was a little surprising—the yoals were unique to northeast Oun, she'd learned during her very first year in the Palace library. Had his father hailed from here?

"Tell me when we're far enough out." Aison's voice was rough; startled out of her thoughts, Darya's head jerked up. His face was averted, but a muscle jumped in his jaw. Clearly he wanted nothing more than to shove her overboard, preferably bound hand and foot. "Are you even listening to me?" he snapped, still staring determinedly away from her.

That almost surprised a nervous giggle out of her—and what terrible timing that would have been; he probably *would* shove her overboard if she laughed in his face. "Yes, I'm sorry—yes, we're out far enough."

Aison lashed the sail down firmly, locked the yoal's single wide oar into its ring, then turned around to look her full in the face. "Who paid you?"

The words made so little sense that for a moment she almost thought he wasn't speaking to her at all—but they were quite alone in the tiny yoal, the calm sea stretching out for leagues in all directions save for the now-distant shore. "What?"

"Who paid you to carry this tale to the Emperor?" Two spots of color burned high on his cheekbones—he was fairer than the Emperor, than Darya herself, fair enough for his temper to show through his skin. "Was it one of his daughters' husbands? Or a great-nephew? You should know they have no care for the tools they use— they're far more likely to discard them than reward them, once their purpose is served. If this is as ridiculous a story as I think it is, I recommend you drown yourself down there before coming back to shore empty-handed. And if you *don't* come back, don't doubt I will look for your body, and if I don't find it, you'd best not show your face anywhere in the Empire. I *will* find you."

Speechless, Darya stared back at him. There was nothing more she could say in the face of such seething hostility. It didn't matter that she herself hadn't been the one to carry the tale of the *salaatu*'s healings to the Emperor; she'd even downplayed every aspect of it that had reached the Emperor's ears, as far as she had dared without causing offense to him, who had been so desperately delighted to hear it at all.

Darya inhaled deeply; Aison shifted back, shoulders stiffening, but she only exhaled hard, then inhaled again, then a third time; his eyes widened, as blue as the Emperor's, the rich deep color of a summer sky in evening. Those eyes were the last thing she saw as she squeezed her own tight shut and thrust herself off the side of the yoal and down into the dark waters.

The shock of the frigid water was painful and the rushing roar of bubbles around the deep impact of her body deafened her. She sank quickly, the weight of her now-soaked smock and kirtle, underlinen and boots dragging her down far faster than she could have swum alone. She began to struggle out of her clothes, shoving the sodden handfuls down and away as fast as she could.

With nothing but her boots left in her hands, her descent slowed to almost nothing. She was deep enough that the daylight world above had shifted into an eerie dimness; she could just make out the bottom of the yoal far above her head, barely the size of the pad of her thumb. She tilted her head down, to look at the pale brown of her arms and legs that were slowly acquiring a smooth, reflective sheen. Her braids waved gently as she drifted in the twilight haze, the weight of the water an implacable cocoon around her.

But she couldn't stay there forever, as weirdly comforting as it was—the tightness in her chest, the need for fresh air, was growing more urgent. She closed her eyes again and focused on the nearly imperceptible shift of tide and temperature rolling over her, as Sayu had taught her to do all those years ago. Yes— *there* was the current that led to the caverns honeycombing the beachrock scattered across Korshun's inlet.

Darya quickly discovered she was no longer as hardy and limber as she'd been as a girl—her muscles, all of them, were burning after a mere ten minutes of steady swimming, and the starved sensation in her lungs had become torture. She whipped her head around, back and forth, searching with eyes that saw more and more clearly the longer she remained submerged—*there*, that deep wall of shadow just ahead—

Darya dove deep, swimming hard, and reached the familiar, seemingly unbroken mass of rock below the shelf just as she thought her lungs were going to burst. She scrabbled at it, awkwardly pulling herself up hand over hand until her fingers abruptly broke through into empty air, then frantically paddled the last few feet up. With a desperate surge of strength flung she herself up over the shelf, head and shoulders finally breaking the surface of the water.

The stone was icy against her bare flesh, gouging into her as she wrenched the rest of her torso atop it, dragging her shaking legs up after her. She rolled over onto her back—for a long, terrible moment it was as if she'd forgotten how to breathe, but then her lungs spasmed convulsively and she sucked in a deep lungful of air. The damp rock walls rising up around her sparkled in the phosphorescent glow of the moss that coated the cavern's stone ceiling, or perhaps it was only in her own eyes—her vision was dimming as the shakes that racked her body grew more violent, then abruptly faded to black along with all conscious thought.

Darya regained consciousness slowly, drawn by a pervasive feeling of warmth; she opened her eyes to a softer, yellower light than the soulless green glow of the sea moss. Someone had built a small fire near the edge of the shelf she'd so laboriously pulled herself upon.

Her vision blurred, cleared, then blurred again; she rubbed her eyes, wincing at the bite of salt. Her head throbbed sharply as she levered herself up onto one elbow. A shadow blocked the firelight; she flinched back, then stilled, eyes opening wide at the sight of a face she hadn't expected to see again in her lifetime. Though she wasn't sure why she hadn't thought Kel might be the one to come—perhaps she hadn't really believed anyone would come at all.

"Thank you," she said, then spat to clear her mouth. "For the fire."

"You're welcome." His accent was heavier than Sayu's had been—though of course Sayu had had every summer for nine years to practice her Imperial Oun with Darya, and Kel had only had the one. He settled back against the stone wall behind him, his eyes fixing on a point past her head.

Darya found herself unable to tear her gaze from his face and entirely missed the next thing he said. "I'm sorry, what?"

"I said, I thought you'd resolved never to return?" He was looking at her once more—she thought, though she'd never been good at reading him, that he might be wary of her in spite of the sardonic edge to his voice.

Darya swallowed against her tight throat. "I need to speak to the *Alii.* If that's possible." She swallowed again and forced herself to meet his eyes. "The Emperor of all Oun desires it."

He grew very still; the firelight reflecting from the few wet drops remaining on his bare shoulders shone like jewels, unmoved even by a breath.

"Well," he said, after a long pause. "The *Alii* it is, then." He began to rise to his feet.

"Wait! Is—who *is* the *Alii*, now?"

He stopped, then lowered himself back down beside her, legs crossed. Something about the question had pleased him, or reassured him—Darya couldn't fathom why, and her head had started to ache again, enough to blur her thoughts. She closed her eyes, and didn't even start when she felt a feather-light touch on her matted braids.

"Rest," she heard him say. "You're still tired. You've been too long away from the sea. When you wake up will be soon enough for the *Alii*."

She obediently laid her head back down; the rock floor didn't seem so unforgivingly hard now. She found his touch inexplicably soothing—and that was very different than it had ever been; once, his touch had unnerved her, then excited her, then finally driven her to a kind of despair when she had finally accepted that he could never be *just* hers, *only* hers —but it had never before soothed her. Exhaustion, or simply the slow march of time across the years and leagues of hard dry land that had separated her from him

—she didn't know, and was too weary now to care.

Kel—Kel had come ashore with Sayu the year Darya turned sixteen. She'd had more trouble slipping out of the house to meet the *salaatu* on the beach that summer than ever before. Her grandfather, as obviously fond as he'd grown of her, never troubled himself about what she did when she wasn't directly before his eyes, but her mother had finally remembered that she had a daughter on the cusp of womanhood. Endless lessons in the kitchen, the buttery, the stillroom—she'd been left little time for Grandfather and the manor library that spring, and she'd been determined that her summer with Sayu wouldn't suffer the same fate.

But Sayu hadn't been alone, that first morning Darya managed to escape the manor. That stopped her in her tracks, on the very edge of the shoreline, because Sayu had never brought anybody else along before. And it was a boy—a few years older than she was, she thought, closer to Sayu's age—but *why*?

Sayu looked uncharacteristically disgruntled. After their usual embrace of greeting, she'd stepped back, scowling over her shoulder at the newcomer. "And this is Kel—who didn't believe I had an Imperial friend! And who was finally brave enough to come with us on the summer journey."

"Only temporarily," the boy said—he seemed unfazed by Sayu's mild hostility. "Just to see the far lands, and the foreign creatures!" He'd grinned unrepentantly down at Darya, then neatly dodged Sayu's shove.

"They're not *creatures*—"

"Well, I admit, she doesn't look like a *creature*. In spite of her odd attire, she looks as if she could—" He hadn't dodged quickly enough a second time and ended up sprawled on the ground, laughing up at them both.

He hadn't come ashore every day with Sayu, but he had more often than not— he'd been openly delighted with everything on land. The beach, the forest, the village —and Darya, it seemed. He'd never done anything inappropriate, never touched her in any unseemly way—but still he *had* touched her, light fleeting strokes of her face and bare arms, shocking her into stillness each time, to his obvious amusement and her deep embarrassment.

Sayu had grown more and more irritable that summer; finally, it had occurred to Darya what the reason might be. She'd stuttered and stammered over asking it. "Is it—do you *like* him, Sayu?"

"Like him?" Sayu had said distractedly. "I suppose—he's well enough—*oh*." After a second or two of astonishment, she'd burst out laughing. Darya smiled back, relieved, but also puzzled as to what was so funny. Then Sayu sobered abruptly. "No, but he likes you." Darya's face had heated. "Yes, he does! And it can't *be* anything and I wish he'd leave you alone. Darya—our men, they're not like yours. Your people—there's a man, and he marries a woman, and that's it, isn't it?"

"Well," said Darya, who had read most of her grandfather's books by then, "that isn't how it *always* goes—"

"It isn't like that at all for us. Ever. Kel —he has his *hoalli*—" Her lips had flattened in frustration. "There isn't even a word in your language for it. Not brothers, not lovers—but yes, that too. Lovers. Sometimes one of them *does* attach himself to a particular woman—but the rest of the *hoalli* won't accept what they can't share in, not for long…you don't understand a word I'm saying, do you?"

"I do, though!" Darya retorted indignantly—but she hadn't, not really.

And then the rest of that summer, and its dreadful, fiery end—her dozing thoughts skipped quickly over the worst of those memories—followed by a fever dream of a gently rocking boat and Sayu's voice in her ear, promising the *salaatu* would make her well, *could* make her well again. Except that it hadn't been a dream at all, as she had realized upon her first awakening, all those years ago, on the distant beach of the *salaatu*'s true home

It had been night, the sky an enormous black bowl arching overhead. She had levered herself up on her elbows, awestruck—she had never seen the sky so unbroken by anything but the endless expanse of dark, rippling waves below it. The ground beneath her bare arms had been soft as powder, gleaming palely in the starlight—it was sand, but not the rough golden-brown of Korshun's shore; it was as light and fragile as winter snow. The breeze had caressed her face, her bare belly and legs, deliciously warm—she had started to sit up, suffused by a sense of well-being so overwhelming she nearly laughed aloud from the joy of it. Then she'd stilled as a dark silhouette rose from the surf lapping gently against the shore, shaking a silver-black spray of water from his long, fair braids.

Kel.

She'd looked down at herself again, in sudden terror—but the burns were gone, her skin as smooth and clear as a baby's. The *pain* was gone. The relief of it rolled over her in a wave of pleasure, an almost physical caress, and when she looked up again, she found Kel had stepped ashore and was gazing back at her, for once without a smile. She'd shifted her weight to begin to stand, delighting in the effortless movement of her body, then had stopped in startlement as a familiar hand had clasped hers. "Wait," Sayu had whispered into her ear—had she been there all along?

But I feel newborn, Darya thought—*I feel like I could do* anything—*anything I wanted, now—*

"Our people are very different." Sayu's grip had tightened. "And yes, you're different now too. But not inside—not in *here*—" and her fingers had lightly brushed Darya's temple.

Darya started awake. The *salaatu*'s beach was gone, replaced by the damp, ugly cavern walls, though it wasn't Kel beside her now. A woman bent over her instead, thick black hair cropped short—cropped for the *Alii*'s headdress, though she was bareheaded now. Eyes as black as her hair gazed down steadily at Darya, expressionless in the flickering light, set in a face with starker bones than Darya remembered. Then the woman smiled ruefully and she was Sayu again, the Sayu that Darya had run to all her life, until the day she'd run away from her instead. Darya closed her eyes against a sudden rush of tears.

"So you've returned," she heard Sayu say—and it *was* Sayu's voice, half-forgotten, but now so familiar in lilt and tone that she could hardly believe she hadn't remembered every nuance of it.

Darya forced her eyes open, blinking hard to clear the unwanted tears away. "That's what Kel said. More or less." She was at too much of a disadvantage, lying curled on her side—she struggled upright, trying not to grit her teeth too obviously at the shrieking protest of every muscle.

"Why?"

Just like Sayu to cut straight to the point. Darya decided to return the favor. "The Emperor wants to meet you," she said, and lifted her gaze up to meet Sayu's once more and surprised a fleeting look of shock lifting her heavy dark brows. "He's ill." As little as the Emperor wanted that fact bandied about, there was certainly no reason not to say it now, here, with Sayu.

"So? I'm sure the Emperor of all Oun has a dozen physicians, or perhaps a hundred. What has that to do with us?" Sayu was fully back in control of herself now, the gleam in her eyes only ironic. "What has that to do with *you*?"

"He's dying," said Darya, starkly; it was harder to say aloud than she had realized it would be. It was nothing anyone had yet said openly in her hearing, and in fact would never have dared, not if they had wanted to go on living themselves. "I don't know of what. I don't even know if it's something you could heal him of. It isn't just old age—he *is* old, of course, which also might pose some difficulty—"

Sayu waved that away, gaze intent. "And so you approached your Emperor— with a fantastic tale of my people, and our great and terrible magic—"

"No." Darya jerked her face away and stared at the pitted, muddy wall behind Sayu's head; the light of moss was washed out by the firelight, rendered dull and ugly in the sputtering flames. "I wouldn't have told him. It would never have occurred to me to tell him. I barely even knew he was ill, much less—anything else. Hardly anyone does." She sucked in a deep, shuddering breath. "I got drunk, one night a few months ago." It was impossible to explain why—she hardly knew it herself; she had never taken too much wine before in her life. She'd been restless, perhaps— more and more restless; her librarial studies had satisfied *some* part of her, the part she had always thought of as the most important part—she had been unused to having time on her hands, as she sometimes found herself having since graduation. "There was someone— someone I was interested in. I doubt he'd had any real interest in me, of course, at least before that night. We were all drinking together, and somehow he and I ended up in a corner alone, and I told him...not the *entire* story, or even much of any story at all..." She trailed off, barely able to speak for shame. "Of course I know why he seemed so fascinated *now*— he was the son of a high-ranking Imperial courtier, he must have known something, overheard something of the Emperor's illness—and of how all conventional treatments seemed useless. *Any* chance of a cure must have seemed worth the chase to him, and after all, what did *he* have to lose by it? So... he began to pursue me." Lightly, casually, yet with enough of an appearance of real engagement behind it that she had fallen for it. Like the most unutterable fool. "He managed to pry rather more details out of me after that. And then *he* went to the Emperor."

The silence that followed was quite miserable, at least for Darya. "I see," she heard Sayu say, finally—but she heard no anger in that voice; startled, she met Sayu's gaze once more. "Well...it wouldn't be an entirely *bad* thing, to have Imperial Oun in our debt." Sayu's lips were faintly curved "Perhaps I should thank you." Darya's own lips parted; her *What?* had no breath behind it—but Sayu understood it well enough. "Let's also say—I think I owe you this. For if your Emperor's *not* healed, it won't go well for you, will it?" She read the answer in Darya's expression. "So." Sayu rose with effortless grace from her crouch, strong slim hand locking around Darya's wrist and pulling her up to her feet as well, steadying her as she swayed at bit. "My mother warned me not to fool around with the Empire, all those years ago, you know. I defied her,

for you. I let Kel indulge himself with you
—"

"You tried to warn me." Not warn her that Kel could never love her, no—but that no man of the *salaatu* could ever love only one woman, could ever love *anyone*, alone, without his *hoalli*. And she hadn't understood anything, until it was too late.

"Not hard enough. Because I *did* want you to stay with us." She squeezed Darya's wrist lightly before letting go. "Come on. Let's see what we can do to salvage this."

Darya wondered what they thought, the Emperor and all his men, when they spied the *salaatu* fleet on the horizon—she didn't know, because she kept her head firmly down and her eyes on the slick dark wood between her bare feet, gripping the edge of the lead boat with white knuckles. No single trading boat, this; the *salaatu* had come in force. A small force, compared to the full military might of the Empire—but still carrying a good three times more *salaatu* than the Emperor's entire camp of followers.

Darya finally dared to peek upward, as the handful of *salaatu* who had jumped easily overboard ran the lead boat to ground. The Emperor and *Loro* Aison stood surrounded by the guards and outriders, their finery strangely artificial-looking under the bright, featureless glare of the overcast sky. Sayu had donned the *Alii*'s fantastic headdress of coral and feathers, and a woven cloth shift that fell halfway to her knees to appease Imperial sensibilities; she graciously accepted the helping hands of her crew as she stepped down onto the beach. Darya felt clumsy as a bear clambering down behind her.

Certainly now was the time for full and formal prostration; the tension emanating from the Emperor's guards was nearly palpable. Darya pushed her way forward and edged around Sayu, who stood proudly in front of the phalanx of *salaatu*. The sand was icy, a thousand tiny sharp knives cutting first into her knees, then into her thighs, belly and chin—she'd had to borrow one of the same thin shifts Sayu now wore, leaving far too much of her skin miserably bare to the elements.

"Sire," Darya said into the sand, muffled but determined. "As you ordered, so I've done—the *salaatu Alii* Sayu stands before you." Sayu had been quite explicit in her refusal to prostrate herself before Imperial Oun.

A long, thick pause, then— "Rise, please, *maya*." The Emperor's voice was noticeably hoarser than it had been before —surprise, or yet another turn for the worse of his health? Darya pushed herself to her feet and fixed her gaze on the Emperor, who thankfully had no attention left to spare for her. The deep mahogany of his flesh had an oddly chalky cast to it, only emphasized by the bejeweled glory of his Court dress; the sleeves of his ornate robes trembled.

Fingers bit into her arm, nearly startling a shriek out of her. Aison was staring down at her with slitted eyes, his mouth barely more than a line bisecting his rigid face. She jerked her head away, though she didn't quite dare do the same with her arm, and fixed her attention back on Sayu and the Emperor.

"—must take place upon our boat," Sayu was saying. *Though better if he came back with us altogether, and stayed for at least the season, just as you did,* she had said to Darya with unusual seriousness, during their boat ride back to the Emperor's camp, *but I think he won't. You agree?* Which had also meant that Sayu wouldn't be able to sing him back to health alone as she had done for Darya, not so far from the *salaatu*'s home, not in the sort of timeframe the Emperor would certainly expect. Hence the boats, plural, of the *salaatu*, in numbers likely never seen before within the boundaries of Imperial waters.

But aside from a brief hesitation, the Emperor seemed unfazed by this comparatively mild demand. "You'll leave your young friend here with my men," he said, with the briefest glance at Darya. Aison's grip tightened brutally on her arm and Darya clenched her teeth together.

"Of course," said Sayu serenely. She offered her hand and the Emperor took it, managing to do so in such a way that almost seemed caressing. Darya didn't think she imagined the appreciation in Sayu's smile. "But—" Sayu's heavy arched brows quirked upward, shifting her smile from pleased to pained all at once, "—she mustn't come to any harm, while we're away?"

"She will not," said the Emperor. "My word on it." He cast another lightning-sharp look back at them—at Aison, this time, Darya realized. She had thought

Aison couldn't possibly look more upset than he already did, but she'd been wrong. Her arm throbbed painfully under the vicelike clamp of his fingers—Darya supposed that degree of harm didn't count.

The Emperor followed the *salaatu* to their dinghy. Minutes later they'd reached the *Alii*'s vessel; three of the *salaatu* assisted the Emperor up its rope ladder with quick light touches and bowed heads. Then he ducked under the low-hanging edge of the *Alii*'s shelter and abruptly vanished from sight. Aison made the faintest of muffled sounds—Darya glanced up at his face, but he'd already turned away and an instant later was hauling her back to the Emperor's tent.

As soon as they reached the half-opened flaps, he thrust her inside, then wheeled around and stalked away, leaving her alone—well, not *entirely* alone; two of the Emperor's personal servants stared round-eyed at her as she stumbled inside. Sand cascaded from her bare legs and feet onto the rich, jewel-toned carpets lining the tent's floor; one of the servant's stares followed it down, then back up, past her short plain skirt to her hair, completely unrestrained and curling wildly over her shoulders and arms from wind and saltwater. Darya turned her back on them and stalked across the tent to the pile of cushions in the farthest corner from the door.

Sleep would have been good for her, but it would not come, even as the light streaming in through the tent flaps gradually faded and the breeze drifting inside the tent took on a cool, bitter edge. As the tent's interior grew darker, one of the servants lit a lantern—just as it flared to life, Aison pushed his way into the tent.

"Out," he said flatly to the servants, who fled without so much as a murmur of protest. Darya recoiled as he strode across the tent and crouched down in front of her, close enough to touch. "If the Emperor doesn't climb back out of that boat at dawn, entirely in one piece and at least as healthy as he was when he first stepped aboard it, you won't die quickly."

Darya was genuinely afraid of the Emperor, whose power over her very life was both whimsical and absolute; she had been genuinely afraid that the *salaatu* wouldn't come to her, in the cavern—but she couldn't fear any such impossible scenario as Aison was clearly imagining. Though at least the reality of their existence had clearly freed him of any conviction he'd had before that she was the agent of some ambitious Imperial relation. "He will," Darya said, spurred into unwilling sympathy for his obvious misery. "Why would they hurt him? What could they possibly gain? The might of the Empire would grind them to pieces if they ever dared show their faces anywhere along the coasts of Oun, ever again."

"You—and *they*—are using him! Using a great man's fear of the only enemy he can't defeat by his strength of will alone—"

The injustice of that was the final straw. Darya's temper, usually mild, had been sorely tried by the events of the past week, and it abruptly snapped. She surged to her feet, kicking the muffling cushions aside, and glared at him. "Oh, yes, they're *using* him! That was their plan all along, when they encamped themselves outside his throne room and forced their way into his presence—"

"*You* were a far more effective messenger!"

"I wasn't any kind of messenger at all! I never wanted to tell his Imperial Majesty anything—I had never so much as *spoken* to him before—"

"And that's what made it all the more effective," Aison ground out. "A whisper, a rumor to amuse him, about some girl nobody knew anything about—carried by a son of the Chancellor himself—"

Darya couldn't help her flinch, or the heat that flooded her face, though if anything it made her even more furious. "Yes, I was a fool to say anything to *anyone*, you can't possibly despise me for that more than I do myself." That part of her that Kel had so thoroughly awakened all those years ago, somehow escaping the iron control she'd kept it under ever since —"You can't think that *this* is what I wanted to come of it!""

"The harm this journey alone has caused him—"

"Then perhaps you should've done a better job of healing him yourself, physician!" she snapped. "Then he wouldn't have been tempted to resort to this, this *charlatanry* in the first place!"

Aison took a single step toward her, his fists clenched, one rising, but Darya was in no mood to indulge him now. *"The Emperor's word!"* she hissed, and he recoiled as if she'd struck him instead of nearly the other way around. His fist dropped back to his sides and anger—and perhaps shame—reddened his cheeks, leaving the skin around his mouth white.

"Whatever lies you told him to convince him of this folly—"

"I only *ever* told him the truth—perhaps he *is* a great man, far greater than you, and knows it when he hears it!" A sob, harsh and ugly, tore itself out of her throat—she'd started to cry, and hadn't even realized it. "I can't prove the healing—they did far too good a job of that —but I can prove to you the price of it. You'll need to know anyway, as the Emperor's *physician.*" Her voice dripped scorn. "Take hold of me, and pinch my nose shut and cover my mouth."

He was taken aback enough by this that his flush faded a little, his hands loosening at his sides. "What?"

"You heard me." He stared blankly at her. "*Do it,* you coward!"

That was enough to spur him; Darya barely had time for one deep breath before he gripped her shoulders roughly, then whirled her around and slammed her back against his chest. His fingers clamped down over her nose as mouth, as unyielding as steel bands.

Her lungs spasmed as the shock of impact tried to force a gasp out of her, and for a long panicked second she thought that perhaps she couldn't do it after all, here on dry land. The change had been easy and painless after she'd jumped from the *yoal*—her body, cradled in the deep implacable grip of the sea, had simply responded to its natural element. But now—

Her lungs spasmed again, then abruptly settled. She relaxed back against Aison, her pulse slowly subsiding in her own ears as her vision began to blur. The seconds ticked past, then a minute—two minutes—her skin grew slick as oil against his hands, wrenching a revolted grunt from him, but his grip didn't loosen. Three minutes—four minutes—five—six— by then, even with her lack of physical exertion, she could feel the first faint burn of starvation in her lungs.

Then he released her. She turned slowly around to face him, gazing up at him with eyes she knew looked utterly inhuman, unbroken ovals of shining pearl like a queen conch's inner shell. Aison took two careful steps away, his own eyes wide and unblinking on her face. She looked back at him for several seconds, still utterly unbreathing—then gently, deliberately inhaled.

"You see," she said.

Shouts outside the tent awoke her—Darya struggled up from the deep carpets, raking the salt-dried mess of her hair out of her face to squint at the tent flaps—still closed, but the light of dawn was creeping in through the gaps in the lacing. A quick glance around the tent confirmed that she was alone. She pushed herself creakily upright; every muscle in her body had stiffened during the night and now screamed in protest. The shouts had ceased, the silence outside the tent now ominous—she staggered over to the flaps and fumbled them open.

The glittering gold reflection of the sun on the ocean briefly blinded her, then resolved into two forms stepping onto shore—a tall, thin man, his hair blazing silver in the sunlight, and a woman nearly as tall as he, long-limbed and graceful, the coiling ends of her headdress whipping around them both in the chill morning wind.

A flurry of movement in Darya's periphery resolved itself into Aison, running forward and stopping abruptly several feet away from the Emperor, who had raised his hand palm-out to halt the headlong rush. "I'm well," said the Emperor—his voice was strong, resonant. The same vibrance that newly infused his voice had infused his face as well—he might have been a man in his fifties, not his seventies. "Aison." The last word was strangely tender. The rising sun shone mercilessly down on Aison's face, now wet with tears.

"Let me examine you, Sire," said Aison. *"Please."*

The Emperor smiled faintly. "Of course." He released Sayu's hand—Sayu was looking at him with an expression Darya found very difficult to read, because she could not believe it. The Emperor and Aison headed for the tent. Darya hurried forward, noting the abortive moves of a few guards towards her, but a dozen *salaatu* suddenly emerged from the surf to plant themselves directly behind their *Alii* and the guards backed away.

"An interesting man, your Emperor," said Sayu, her expression a shade too solemn as she gazed down at Darya's face. "*Very* interesting." Her dark eyes crinkled up at the corners.

Apparently Darya hadn't misread her expression at all. "How *could* you," she said, very faintly, and then, to her complete surprise, choked on a giggle. "He —you—he's *old*, you know—"

"A very Father Wisdom," Sayu agreed serenely. "Just like the Imperial tales you used to tell me."

Then Sayu held out her arms, and Darya fell into them. "I've missed you," Darya said, struck nearly insensible by the truth and strength of it, her voice muffled against Sayu's shoulder.

"And I've missed you." Sayu's voice was very soft. "I didn't know how much I would, until I knew you were gone for good."

"I didn't know if you'd come."

"Always," said Sayu. "I'll always come." She paused. "If you're where I can even reach you. Darya, perhaps you ought to stay with us, this time?"

"I understand why you're asking," Darya said slowly. "And...I can't promise that I won't have trouble now, going forward." Her mouth twisted. "Perhaps I'll become a favorite of the Court—"

"Or perhaps you'll end up dead." Sayu's lips flattened. "Consider—"

"No," said Darya. "I can't."

"That Kel," Sayu muttered. "I *told* him —" Kel hadn't returned to the Emperor's camp with her and Sayu. She'd been glad and sorry, hurt and relieved, and supposed dismally that she'd never truly get over him.

But— "It isn't just what happened with Kel." The Imperial library—she thought of it now, dry and warm with its hundreds of shelves of books, paper and ink, the infinite well of knowledge and discovery contained within its depths. Of her grandfather, his arms around her, holding her burnt and seeping body as if it were fragile as glass, carrying her to the *salaatu*'s boat in the dead of night so the rest of the family wouldn't try to stop him. "I can't—too much of me is here." Her chin jerked involuntarily over her shoulder, past the tents, towards the manor house looming silently on its hill "In the *Empire.* I *can't* leave that. Not for good. Not forever." Darya took a deep breath. "But I was stupid to try to do the same with you—to leave you, leave the *salaatu* forever, leave... myself, what I became. As much as anything else, *that's* why I ended up being dragged back here, and then dragging *you* into this, this Imperial *mess*—"

"Now *that*," said Sayu, dark eyes alight, "is...what is the word? Irreverent? Or no, you don't actually worship your Emperor, your dives into the sand at his feet notwithstanding." She sobered abruptly, keen gaze searching Darya's. "But I do hope that means what it sounds like." One corner of Sayu's mouth curved up. "Because I may have suggested to him that he should return here himself, every year or so...just for a brief visit, just to monitor his continued health—and that he should also perhaps bring someone along, someone familiar with my people, when he does so—"

Darya's lips parted, but no sound emerged. Could it be that easy? *Could* she return, every year—with Imperial favor, even approval...? She thought of Aison and shivered involuntarily—she didn't think *he* at least would let everything go, let bygones be bygones...but he would never oppose the Emperor's will. She was sure of that.

Sayu nodded once, sharply, then gave Darya's shoulders a final squeeze before she released her. Darya stepped back as Sayu turned away and waved her *salaatu* into their dinghies. They all rowed out to the *Alii*'s vessel. She watched the smaller boats flock to its side, like chicks to their mother; then the broad triangular sails caught the sharp morning wind, the forest of oars splashed down and churned, and it surged away, a rapidly shrinking silhouette against the risen sun.

See Lisa Short's story "Salaatu" online at Metaphorosis.
If you liked it, leave a comment. Authors love that!
Remember to subscribe to our e-mail updates so you'll know when new stories are posted.

About the story

This story actually takes place in a secondary fantasy world I created—Metaphorosis published the first story I wrote in it ("The Season of Withering", October 2019)]. Though the Emperor of the country the characters lived in is only briefly mentioned in that story, I became rather interested in him, then interested in setting more stories in that world, and even in the exact same time frame, just geographically separated. I have another short story (possibly a novella) in the works set in the southwestern reaches of the Empire (same time frame, though, again) and my in-progress novel is also set in this world and time, though on an entirely different continent. The

Emperor is still only a secondary character in "Salaatu", but we do become more acquainted with him as seen through the eyes of the story's protagonist—and I also wanted to write a story that included a non-subjugated people coexisting with a large, heavily structured political entity, and not the story of their subjugation either—a story that demonstrates their strength and independence from the looming behemoth of Empire.

A question for the author

Q: What other writers inspire you?

A: Authors that inspire me—when I first started to answer this question, I realized about halfway through that what I was listing were authors whose stories I loved—not that there's anything wrong with that! But not necessarily authors who inspired me. Now, I do love the following authors' stories too, but their work also leaves me daydreaming for hours and aspiring to emulate their levels of creativity, artistry and/or originality: Octavia Butler, Rivers Solomon, Joan Slonczewski, Robert E. Howard, Barbara Hambly, and Tanith Lee.

About the author

Lisa Short is a Texas-born, Kansas-bred writer of fantasy, science fiction and horror. She has an honorable discharge from the United States Army, a degree in chemical engineering, and twenty years' experience as a professional engineer. Lisa currently lives in Maryland with her husband, youngest child, father-in-law, two cats and a puppy. She is a member of SFWA and HWA.

lisashortauthor.com, @Lisa_K_Short

There was enough left of the stairs for the Curator to warily make their way up a level — to the outside viewing platform — and gaze up at the hole in the sky. *How strange for there to be no tomorrow.*

The Curator stopped humming their song, reflected on the oddness of the thought. *Should I feel sad?* they thought. *Even anger would be appropriate.* But they'd shed their biological body eons ago, to fulfill a duty deeper than flesh, and any emotion was impossible. Nevertheless, they had long been aware of a certain *emptiness*, a lingering sense of having *failed.* Just as they had failed to keep another promise made on a distant summer afternoon for the sake of another fruitless dance.

Over the millennia since that day, one half of the stellar binary had tumbled towards its hungrier, heavier twin. Now, beneath the swirling, glowing disc of particles that had once been a sun, no eternity remained. Instead, the Archive world surged and bulged with liquified rock as it broke apart. The last dawn had come and gone. This evening, the sun would inevitably set for the last time before it — and the world it had once supported — became dust.

No one had come to the Archive. The People were forgotten, and the Curator's life had — at the end of everything — been in vain. *Today is proof the universe cannot abide forever.*

"I am, perhaps, the last sentient mind in the universe," the Curator said, dutifully dictating the speculation into the records, for no-one to hear.

"Thee was most totally, never," said an unexpected voice.

It took the Curator several seconds to interpret the signal as a mutated, clumsy, single tone form of their own language. Confused, they looked around, traced the sound to a shape in the doorway. A figure with an unfamiliar number of limbs, sealed inside some form of... exoskeleton? Environment suit? Surely the shape was the hallucination of a wishful thought; just a damaged circuit in the depths of the Curator's worn out and patched brain.

"Greetings, Formal Neuter," continued the strange creature, bending awkwardly in the middle. "Canyons of >ERROR, NOT FOUND< with taking an excess of forward transition."

The Curator could not believe the reliability of the sensory input they received. *Is this an alien? Here? Now?* How had it got here? The Curator accessed the Archive's sensors and found — in the static of overloads and exceeded parameters — an outlier datum in the vicinity of the roof, barely minutes old. *A ship!*

"Do give me a moment," said the Curator, calmly and politely. Somewhere in the recesses of the Curator's mind, they hoped the Visitor had some technology or magic to save the Archive. They struck up the cheerful hum again. "I need to compensate for linguistic drift and your frankly terrible accent."

The Visitor gestured with its upper limbs in a way that did not seem threatening, and the Curator hastily processed. Systems unused for a billion years responded to the Curator's summons, and a side routine brought light to the reading room and images to its long-dull screens. The Assistant's yelp of surprise carried through the conduits. Below, the reactor shuddered in time with the convulsing planet, and gave all it could.

"I'm sorry I took so long," the Visitor said, as the Curator accommodated the transformed words. It lacked tonal nuance, but that was also to be expected.

"I am sorry too," said the Curator. "The Archive is at your disposal, comprising seven thousand physical artefacts, plus six hundred and eighty-four billion zettabytes of data."

The Visitor tipped what might have been a head upward at the particulate sky. "I don't think I can stay that long."

"You have storage? On your ship? You can take much with you…"

"I … can't. The drive takes up so much space. It has to — to resist that." The figure waved a limb toward the bright ring and its dark core.

The last of the Curator's hope shattered in that moment. *Then why did you even come?* the Curator thought, only to realize too late they had spoken it aloud.

"I wanted you to know you weren't alone," the Visitor said. "To tell you I've followed pieces of your history across a thousand planets. I wanted to promise that your people are remembered."

"But not all of us. Not everything," said the Curator. Overhead, brilliant white gasses swirled towards oblivion.

"No," said the Visitor. "Not everything. But perhaps you could choose something special?"

The Curator thought for many milliseconds. They thought of science, biochemistry, anatomical structures. They thought of brilliant crystalline buildings that murmured in the heat of a warm day. But the laws of the universe were universal, bodies had ceased to matter long ago, and the houses were long gone. Then they thought of a sunlit afternoon and a lover's chirping limbs as they whirled around the square, and a promise unkept.

"I wonder," said the Curator, eventually. "If you would have time to visit the music section."

The world ended exactly six hours and thirty-eight minutes later.

The Visitor had, some three thousand seconds ago, climbed into its ship, humming the song the Curator had taught it. They watched it go, watched engines of unfathomable design carry the People's last wish in the form of as many crystals as the Visitor could fit in the pockets of its suit — to a young species in an older universe. One song, one thousand years of music, and one lover's gift, never given, on a faraway summer day.

The Curator found just enough energy inside themselves to crawl down the crumbling stairs. They left a leg or two behind — but they didn't need to patrol anymore, didn't need to pay attention to counting. Simply one final duty to keep.

In the disintegrating remnant of the reading room, the Curator (the first and the last) contentedly delivered their terminal speech to a half-working librarian and the Assistant. The Assistant stopped polishing, for one long second, to applaud. Flared brightly for a second more as the particles that had once been the Archive, and the Assistant, and everything else, began their final and near eternal descent into the black hole.

The Curator hummed contentedly and returned to dance in the warmth of the sun.

See Sam Griffin's story "Hard Sunset" online at Metaphorosis.
If you liked it, leave a comment. Authors love that!

Remember to subscribe to our e-mail updates so you'll know when new stories are posted.

About the story

The first version of the story came from one of the creative challenges my partner (graphic/web designer and photographer) and I sometiimes set each other. Write a story in an afternoon, and they'd come up with some kind of art for it. This prompt was 'sunset'...

I like to subvert prompts — I'm annoying like that — and I'd been watching a science documentary about the universe. Can't get much more sun or setting or going down than a black hole!

From there on, a swirl of Brian Cox, Arthur C. Clarke, Douglas Adams and a sniff or two of a certain long running Brit SF show led to the Curator, the Archive, and a tale of the last day. But that's only where it began.

In the four years between the first version and the published version, I'd finally received a decent level of cPTSD therapy. In edit for *Metaphorosis*, I could properly engage the Curator's emotions. Now the story is consciously infused by neurodivergence, loss, purpose, legacy, finding peace with the past, and making sense of endings. And hope, of course, which rarely looks quite how you expect...

A question for the author

Q: Do you live near where you were born? Have you traveled much?

A: My home in the North West UK is less than 60 miles from where I was born, which is probably not far enough (or close enough!) to be interesting. Home contains my partner and my cats, with the luxury of a big garden and a nearby beach, so no complaints!

My travelling is mostly of the mental variety ... which is a) cheaper, b) more disability friendly, and c) comes with less (but not zero) chance of losing my passport. Also, many more possible destinations, unconstrained by space, time, or reality. Honestly, I have been on exactly two aeroplanes in my life and hated it — I'm not a fan of being up anywhere. Luckily I do like rugged scenery, rain on canvas, history and lukewarm weather, as I'm spoiled for all those in Britain. If everything aligned for a big trip, I'd love to go to Norway (for the Aurora), but until that time bring on the words!

About the author

As a neurodivergent, queer, and disabled author of speculative fiction, Sam is many things. An academic, creative, middle-aged rebel, a problem solver and chaotic mess. Her/ their recurring themes include liminality, becoming, entropy, being truly seen, and sex.

www.unquietwords.co.uk

Translations for a Dead Sea

Corey Farrenkopf

Laura struggled to hold a half dozen nails between her lips. She'd found the hammer under the sink, along with several rudimentary tools her father had used for cabin maintenance. He had never been very handy. She used her knee to balance the plywood, galvanized steel chilling her tongue. Once the wood was aligned over the first window facing the sea, she leaned a shoulder onto the salt-worn surface, pressing it in place as she drove a nail into the casement. The hammer clatter reverberated in light fixtures and summer screens, a metallic chittering not dissimilar to cicadas.

She repeated the process until the graying wood was tacked in place.

The next board waited beneath the deck. Her father had cut each to the exact dimensions of corresponding windows, eight in all. The only window he left unadorned was the leaky, western-facing skylight. Even though the roof wasn't steep, her father hated ladders, so it was left bare to view every winter snow and swelling Nor'easter. The cabin was only meant for three season habitation, the insulation thin. Everyone in the area boarded up for winter, to keep out storm winds and the freezing spittle rising off the ocean.

"Isn't it a little early to be putting up the boards?" Ray asked from behind her. Ray was in his early forties, a thick brown beard covering his face, eyes the color of the sea, wardrobe composed of nothing but flannel.

"Definitely not," Laura replied, words struggling around the nails.

"I'd say we have at least a month of good weather ahead. Won't you miss the view?"

Laura didn't know how to answer honestly, so she lied.

"It'll help me concentrate when I'm translating. If I spend too much time looking at the water, I'm going to get nothing done."

"How is the writing going?" Ray asked, moving to her side, steadying the plywood with a callused hand.

Ray lived in one of the large renovated ranches across the street. He worked as a maintenance man for the stretch of cabins crowding the road, for summer people incapable of fixing toilets or hooking up propane tanks. They'd known each other for years, only growing close after his wife passed, leaving him with their twin daughters and the ever encroaching sea.

"It's going," Laura replied. "A few more weeks and I'll be pretty close to the end."

"Your dad would have been proud, finishing it up for him like that," Ray said as Laura hammered another nail. She slipped, aim off, spilling a cascade of galvanized steel across the deck from her toolbelt. Laura swore as the two bent to retrieve the sharpened metal. She'd heard too many horror stories of thin soled sneakers and lockjaw to leave the nails for long.

"Who's to say? I don't think he even knew if it *should* be finished," Laura said once the stray nails were gathered.

Ray looked at Laura askew, then shrugged, going back to holding the wood.

"Well, I'm sure he would be," Ray said.

Her father's cottage was identical to the fifteen other white, clapboard cottages strung along the road in North Truro, one of the towns farthest out on the Atlantic-wrapped peninsula. Neighboring roads repeatedly washed out with sand, blacktop giving way to soft shoulders, desert-like. Sparse forests of scrub pine pressed up to the dunes, the scent of sap always on the air.

Each building was a single story. Turquoise shutters framed windows. Chimneys divided rooflines. Over their shoulders was Cape Cod Bay, a thin stretch of beach on the opposite side of a concrete seawall. When storms rolled in, roiling waves kicked about front steps, the buildings more aquatic than terrestrial. In October, most were abandoned, the seasonal economy come and gone for the year.

Ray said only eccentrics stuck around.

Laura welcomed the epithet. She had a goat tattoo on her collarbone, had given up dying the gray out of her bangs. She used to stitch patches of band names to leather jackets, fixing studs to shoulders. She was getting too old for that, though, she told herself.

Laura had lost her previous lease in Boston when she could no longer afford the rising rent. It was hard to afford anything in the city when you were single, and after an unpleasant divorce in her late twenties, owning her own place always seemed like a distant daydream. The cottage was her only option, the mortgage already paid. All she had to worry about were taxes and insurance. After the prolonged pandemic, her job, like many, had cut hours and gone remote. The cottage got decent wifi. It was enough to continue her graphic design work, sketching logos for organic juice shacks, crafting tri-folds for some corporation's overpriced healthcare package.

Her job didn't really matter anymore. It paid the bills, kept the heat on, provided enough for takeout twice a week, but little else. It was her nightly task that propelled her days. Her father, an armchair academic after a lifetime of marine biology, had left behind a poetic text he believed held the secret to many things. He had believed the words could provide hope, a tipping point, some great revelation and unveiling. But he also believed the inverse, possibly one of the reasons he hadn't made it through the sheets of paper now piled on Laura's writing desk.

With the boards up, her view was gone, the ocean curtained by plywood, the desk lit only by the warm glow slipping beneath the lampshade. Now the windows only peered at the backside of graying boards, several dark knots like wide eyes gazing back at her while she wrote, fingers tracking through dictionaries, unheard voices muttering in her ear.

She hadn't wanted to cover the glass, but she didn't have many choices.

They'd get in if she didn't provide a barricade. From the noises she had heard, her sunless rooms were a small price to pay to sequester her from what came in the night.

Laura had written a pros and cons list for finishing the translation of her father's found poem.

CONS:

There are still a few trees.

Cori and Mark. Diane. Russel and Taraneh. Cashel, Daria, Ralph. Gabrielle.

Art's thriving.

There are still guitars. Concerts every weekend.

All those retired ladies at the conservation trust.

The girls.

Ray

PROS:

There are only a few trees.

Most people disappoint me.

Most people don't care about other people, or animals, or plants…especially not plants.

Colony collapse disorder.

Rising ocean temps.

The Sixth Extinction.

Death hornets.

Favorite Indian restaurant closed.

Laura's father, while being good with words, had never been the best translator, hence the unfinished manuscript and the age-muddled line he believed could be understood in one of two ways:

Once rewritten, all will be calm and well
or
Once rewritten, none shall remember calm that well

Laura looked at it as a fifty-fifty chance. Pleasant improvements or vague unpleasantries? She didn't know the scale, what extent of healing or joy or despair would come from the fractured lines. The way things were going, those were decent odds. Speeding up the apocalypse wasn't a great option, but continuing on the same trajectory would lead to blight, emptiness, and very little potable water. Laura wasn't very good with knives or machetes, so defending the only clean waterhole for miles seemed like a grim prospect. She'd read the emergency reports, the UN's 2029 predictions and warnings. Local governments were already talking about placing water restrictions on communities, about storing surplus runoff in newly constructed holding tanks isolated from the public. It was never too early to think about where your next drink might come from, her father had always said.

The thought was never far from her mind.

Her father had bought the crumbling papyrus from an indoor flea market in Maine. He'd found it nestled in a poster-tube between a taxidermied armadillo and a glass case containing antique pearl-handled revolvers. It was in Greek, the language of his great-great grandfather. Laura had sprung for the Rosetta Stone app for the two of them, promising they'd learn in tandem. It was a point of bonding. He hadn't been doing well since her mother passed, and the daily lessons gave them an easy entry point for conversation. Once she became fluent, her father had promised he'd bring her to Athens.

They had been at the translation for four years, moving between a pile of dictionaries and the app, before lung cancer caught him.

Now it was up to her to figure out the words left behind.

Once dusk had settled, a resonant thud quivered through the plywood. Laura's eyes left the half-composed paper, drifting to the hammer she'd left on the table by the door. The door itself was the only point of entry to the cabin. She couldn't board it up and still make it to the store when she needed eggs and milk and basic human contact. She had to hope the new twin deadbolts Ray had installed would hold. It had been a strange request to make, needing two, but Ray seemed to understand the fears of a woman living alone.

There was also the unprotected skylight, but the thing (things?) outside seemed to have no skill in climbing, so Laura pushed the second point of entry from her mind. It would have been even weirder to ask Ray to install another latch up there, or some heavy-duty screen, though she knew he'd be more than happy to do it for her. Ray seemed more than happy to do most things for Laura and that made her glad. After her divorce and five years of on-again-off-again online dating, she had begun to wonder if there were any decent guys left out there.

Decent was only one of many words Laura could think of to describe Ray.

Another thud snaked through the boards, followed by the sound of claws dragging along their surface. Something circumnavigated the outside of the cottage, slender fingertips mapping the borders between her life and theirs. She was still trying to figure out if there was more than one. A flock? A gathering? A parliament? Laura didn't know. She'd only caught glints that first night before she put up the boards. Only the teeth stayed with her, the sight of moonlight catching on enamel.

Either each night they grew more determined at forcing their way in, or there were more of them. More claws scraping at boards, more feet/flippers/tails scuffing along the deck. Whenever she made progress on the translation, the clamoring grew worse, as if each new word called to them more persistently.

The real problem was whether they were the hero or the villain of the story. Had they come to stop her from finishing the manuscript, halting her from destroying the world, saving the human race from an endless dark horizon? Or were they something else entirely?

Her father's field of study had been mollusks.

"They're nature's healers," he'd once said to Laura over Thai food, a dinner date of broken Greek underway. "Did you know that one oyster can filter fifty gallons of water a day? We've been trying to find a way to use them to clean up waste in the bay."

"I didn't know that," Laura replied, though she had. It was her father's favorite factoid about his work, most of which was too jargon-heavy for her to follow. But the oysters she understood.

The oysters were one of the reasons her father had fallen so hard into the translation. Their shells were growing thin. Ocean acidification ate away at them slowly year after year. If the trend continued, they would eventually become translucent, like pebble ghosts scattered across the floor of the bay. Then a year or two after that, they'd be dead.

"So you want to save the world for oysters?" Laura asked him one night as he hunched over his papers, lamp bleeding green through its banker's shade.

"What's good for oysters, is good for fish, is good for gulls, is good for us. It's all connected."

"I think I'm going to blame vandals," Laura said as Ray examined the shreds of plywood heaped beneath the bay-side windows, a harsh tear dividing the top of the wood from the bottom.

Wind was heavy off the water, a salt sting in the air, their skin peppered by sand. A tumbleweed of a hydrangea head rolled into the dunes, the once blue bloom now decaying brown.

Ray picked up the larger half of the plywood, fingers running along the gashed surface.

"Vandals?" he asked. "Would have thought me and the girls would have heard something. I guess the ocean's been pretty rough lately. Hard to hear anything over all those waves."

"Yeah, let's go with vandals. Who else would do this?"

Laura knew very well who would do this.

Or vaguely well.

Or just vaguely.

She hated lying to Ray, but didn't know how else to explain her current circumstances, poetry summoning potential demons and all.

"If the vandal was a tiger, maybe, but we don't have many of them out here," Ray replied. "I chased off a pack of coyotes a few weeks back, but nothing bigger than those guys."

"So, if it wasn't vandals, or tigers, or coyotes, what would you put your money on?" Laura helped him slide a new piece of wood from the back of his truck, hoping that Ray might know more than he was letting on.

"Have you pissed anyone off lately?"

"I haven't talked to anyone besides you and the girls and a few people at the grocery store in the last month. I might've pissed off one of those retired bagging ladies who's never careful with my eggs, but otherwise, nope."

"Do you have a gun?" Ray asked.

Laura almost dropped her end of the plywood.

"Do you think I need one?"

"Whatever ripped this guy down," he said, gesturing towards the scrap wood, "is big. Biggish at least. People in the Outer Cape get eccentric sometimes. Who knows if someone bought an exotic pet and it's been getting out at night. You know, real Tiger King shit. That's the only thing I can think of. Would you like a gun? On loan of course."

"Can you legally give me a gun?"

"Don't worry, cops aren't going to come around to bother you. In the off season, they're on call, mostly. And if you shoot something, I'll come running and say I did it. Problem solved. It's not like I'm going to miss a gunshot in the middle of the night."

"Is it safe?"

"Of course. Do you think I'd keep guns in the house around the girls otherwise?"

"Well, if that's the case, yes, I'd very much like a gun."

"It's all yours. You sure there's nothing else to tell?" Ray said, pointing to the wood. "I really can't imagine sleeping through all this."

"Earplugs do wonders," Laura replied, unable to meet Ray's eyes, pretty sure he'd never glimpsed what slipped from the sea nightly.

Later that night, Laura lay next to Ray beneath the covers of his queen-sized bed, staring out towards her cottage through the open window, waiting for inarticulate shadows to swarm her doorway. She hadn't left her translation inside. She knew better. It rested in her backpack by the bedroom door. A copy of the first page lay on her writing desk back in the cabin, the lure hopefully singing to those amorphous shapes slouching from the sea.

The night was still early, the girls having gone to sleep after an impromptu ping-pong tournament with Laura. They'd fallen into the custom of batting the hollow ball back and forth most evenings, something to unwind after a long day of school (for the girls) and dread (for Laura).

Somehow, Laura and Ray managed to keep their sex quiet, never waking his daughters, for which she was thankful. Ray's work-toned body was slick with sweat beside hers, one damp arm slung around her waist as he snored into their pillows. He had fallen asleep quick. He'd been rebuilding a neighbor's deck all week. She didn't fault him. It was just nice to not be alone for a few hours, to hear someone else's breath besides her own.

Laura's mind tracked to her pros and cons list, all that would be lost if she were wrong, Ray's name down there at the bottom. The girls. She always wrestled with the same issue before sleep. It was only after dark she doubted her purpose, fearful of mistakes, of losing those she loved.

But those she loved would be lost anyway, just on a later date when tides had risen and cannibalism wasn't so frowned upon.

Laura thought of the sections as cantos; she'd been obsessed with Dante's *Inferno* when she was an undergrad and always liked to think of section breaks in poetry as such. She knew that wasn't accurate, but who was there to correct her? Ray wasn't the reading type and the girls hated anything that resembled homework.

According to Laura's calculations, she was on canto twenty-two of thirty.

It went like so:

By the water I have written.
Several days have passed.

*They swim far out. Farther than I
might swim.
I don't swim.
I fear what I see on the surface.
I fear what lies below.
If there is no name, it doesn't exist.
I fear I will find the words to describe
it.
To call it into life, plucked from my
head,
dropped at my feet, writhing limbs
and teeth.
I'm often tempted to lay down my
pen.
To forfeit these lines.
But it is also these lines that keep
them in the water.
But it is also these lines that call
them ashore.*

Laura kept the gun within reach. She left
the hammer by the door. She'd seen many
horror movies; she knew to tuck plenty of
weapons away. A crowbar by her bedside,
the tire iron from her trunk beneath the
pull-out couch, a scaling knife behind the
television. Two steps and she could be at

any hiding place. She wasn't sure most of the objects would do much against what she'd seen through the cracked plywood, but it was better than nothing.

The night she had spent in Ray's bed, the creatures had left her cabin alone, as if they knew she wasn't inside, as if they knew she wasn't dragging pencil across paper, thumbing through dictionaries for difficult adjectives. Was it the words that called to them or the work that led to the words? Laura hated not knowing, hated the uncertainty of every aspect of her life, both environmentally and romantically speaking. She didn't know if Ray saw her as anything more than a fun hookup, if he imagined they had a future together, if he'd willingly do all the macheteing to keep their joint water supply safe.

She was trying to work up the nerve to ask, but the timing didn't seem right.

Nothing really seemed right anymore.

Three days later, the moon hung nearly extinguished above Laura's cabin, a pale sliver in the overshadowed sky. It cast enough light to make out the teeth, the slap of gums, a tongue tasting the air as if premeditating its next meal. The thing (things?) had pulled down one of the boards, wrenching the nails from their tired hold. The creature lingered for a moment before moving to the next window, talon-fin-fingers scrambling at the boards as if it were blind, as if some other sense guided it to her home.

It gave her comfort to think the creatures weren't intelligent. They had the opening, the glass right before them, her soft skin just beyond that. But instead, they moved to the next window, repeating the previous process. Laura promised herself she wouldn't shoot until they broke through, until she could smell their breath, feel the heat on her neck. If she shot now, she'd have to explain the thing's corpse to Ray, and the police, and every gawker who swarmed the cottage once a photo landed online. If that was the case, she'd have to confess what she was doing, and someone more knowledgeable would take it out of her hands. Laura didn't want that.

The translations were the only thing that made her feel close to her father anymore, the only thing that gave her life purpose. Designing Kale Chip flyers for her day job certainly wasn't cutting it.

As Laura dropped to the next line of text, which she roughly translated as *There will be joy once collapse. Different joy, but joy nonetheless*, she felt as if her father's hand pressed her shoulder, cold fingers gripping her collarbone. His negative image reflected in the glass, his thin face and beard tinted gray, translucent. Laura reached her free hand up, to place it on his, but there was only gooseflesh coursing down her neck, the call of the wind rushing outside, the stomp and drag of the creatures' movements across the deck. His face slipped from the glass, dissolving back into the writhing night beyond, back into her insomnia-addled memory.

At some point after midnight, Laura heard a splash, something dropping back into the ocean. She had put her pen down moments before and retreated to the mattress, pulling the blankets up around her ears. She prayed sleep would come.

There were only three more pages to translate. Two more cantos.

It wouldn't be long until she knew which version of her father's predictions was true.

"Tigers again?" Ray asked.

It was the fourth time he'd helped rehang the plywood. It was December. The Cape was quiet and gray, the sky low, beach grass freezing in the dunes, their brittle skin snapping like tin bells on windy mornings.

"I think of them as cougars, but that's just me. Tigers are expensive. Cougars are the value point big cat," Laura replied, nails under her tongue.

"Don't you think you should winterize the place, move somewhere inland? Maybe the tigers will leave you alone."

Ray had offered to call the police, or animal control, several times. Each time, Laura refused. She couldn't risk interruption to her work, no more than she already added with her visits with him and the girls.

She'd started to hear her father's voice, reading over the lines, suggesting changes. They were close. Another few days and the oysters wouldn't become living ghosts, another name relegated to the endangered species lists.

"That's not going to help," Laura said.

"You could always stay with me," Ray replied, looking back towards his own home. "The girls would love that."

If she said yes, she knew she'd never finish the translation.

"I'm fine here. For now anyway. Who knows what the future holds? For now, if we fix the windows, that should be enough. The pattern's worked so far. I just need another week, tops, another week—"

"Another week for what? You want to tell me what's going on?"

Laura bit her lip. "It's nothing. Just another day or so and I'm done with dad's old translation, that travelog from the Greek monk I told you about. It's mostly recountings of wildlife, lots of utopic scenery and descriptions of tropical fruit."

Ray nodded uncertainly, as if her words had slipped past him too fast to be believed.

"And what does that have to do with your little night visitors?"

Laura froze. "They must love poetry. It's in high demand." She tried to laugh off the comment, but the forced mirth died in the air between them.

"I see," Ray replied, eyes drifting back towards his house where the girls were playing basketball in the side yard. He began backing away, moving towards the road. He didn't offer to hold the plywood like usual, leaving Laura to use her knee and shoulders. She thought about calling after him, explaining everything, but she didn't want Ray to become a greater deterrent, one of those halting forces, a potential casualty.

But she also didn't want to drive him away, swept out of her life by a torrent of unhinged speculation.

Ray paused before he crossed the street.

"Are you still planning on joining us for dinner tonight?" he called to her. "We're doing lasagna."

"If I can get enough work done," Laura said, a spark of hope floating in her chest. Maybe everything really could be healed, happy endings not solely relegated to fiction.

"Door will be open. Just come over around six if you can. The girls will miss you if you skip out."

Laura had found her father, weeks after the diagnosis, crying before the aquarium in his living room, a holdover from lab days. The bottom was cluttered with mollusks: oysters and clams, mussels adhered to pieces of driftwood in the corner. Streams of green kelp drifted in the artificial current. The buzz of the filter burbled over his sobs.

His forehead was pressed against the glass when Laura pulled up a chair.

"We're definitely not going to make it to Greece," he said.

"We can still go. There's plenty of…"

"Not if I'm going to finish the poem."

"I thought you weren't sure whether that was the right move?"

"I need to leave something behind. Something that will help, otherwise it's all been a waste."

Laura's hand moved to her father's shoulders, rubbing circles into the fabric of his shirt.

"You did plenty of good, Dad. Think of the bay cleanup. Or the dovekie rehab. Or the plover monitoring sites. There's quite a list."

"But it's not enough," he replied.

"Is there ever enough?" she asked.

"I'd hope so."

They remained seated in the dim light of his living room, listening to the burble of the fish tank, observing the subtle movements of the mollusks, her father's entire life's work condensed to a single fifty-gallon tank and a stack of pages.

Laura hadn't left the lights on, certainly hadn't left the door unlocked, not with the completed manuscript on the desk, those final lines ready for recitation. But the cottage was wide open, light bleeding through the skylight and the singular window whose boards had been partially sheared away in the night, the things having left before shattering glass, only tearing the screen to tatters.

It was the closest they'd come to getting in.

Laura had a half dozen donuts clutched in one hand, a bottle of hand-pressed grapefruit juice in the other. She figured she deserved a treat before the end...or the beginning, whatever came after her reading by the water.

The manuscript was exact in its instruction:

*These words must be spoken in sight of the
sea,
over waves,
carried on tides,
washing low to all ears.*

Did oysters have ears? she'd wondered as she wrote, a skip of joy in her throat. That joy deflated as she hesitantly opened the cottage door, holding the donuts before her like a shaking, gluten-heavy shield. She wished she had the gun, or the hammer, or the knife, anything beyond a box of cheap baked goods.

Ray sat on the couch, manuscript pages stacked neatly besides him, the last left in his hand as his eyes traced the remaining words.

"How'd you get in?" she asked, putting down the donuts on her small dining table.

He raised a keyring from his lap without looking up from the page. "You gave me the spares when I installed the locks, remember?"

"That tracks, but why are you here? It's not like the pages call to you like they call to them," she replied.

Ray lifted a small shoulder bag with a patch depicting a goat-headed god and the name of a metal band sewn to the fabric. "You left this last night."

Laura hadn't been able to resist the lasagna.

"Can you just put those down? I worked really hard on them and I can totally explain what they all mean and…"

"I don't know if there's much to explain. The text is pretty straight forward on our options," Ray said, finally looking up, eyes red as if he'd been crying moments ago. "Are you actually going to read this? Have you thought about what it might mean for my girls if it's real? What it means for you and me?"

"If I don't read that, your daughters are going to be murdering neighbors for a bottle of water. Do you really want to be looking over your shoulder the rest of your life waiting for someone to do the same to them? There's no more ping-pong in the apocalypse. No sleepovers. No love. That's what's ahead."

"You don't know that," Ray replied, hand slowly moving through his beard. Over her shoulder, the sun had begun to set, the shortest day of the year only a week away. Winter's chill rushed through the open door, the lap of the sea failing to soothe the tension.

"Some people don't believe science, but I'm not one of them. Neither was my father," Laura said.

"There's always hope…always other options. Your father was real big on hope."

"This was the last thing he wanted." Laura didn't know how true that was, but the words came with confidence. She had to do this for him, after that night by the fish tank.

Before Ray could reply, the sound of something sloshing out of the water crept through the open door, wet and bulky, shifting its weight through the sand. Laura swore, rushing back to the door and slamming it shut, turning the twin deadbolts in place. Ray and Laura held each other's gaze from across the room before their eyes drifted to the unboarded window. A shadowed figure stood there, dripping seaweed from its massive frame. Laura didn't really know what she was looking at. The thing's body was amorphous and many limbed, barnacle-crusted, its head too high to view through the small opening.

"Not tigers," Ray said, eyes wide.

"Not tigers," Laura replied.

"Do you still have that gun?"

"What? Like I'd throw it in the ocean or something with this thing hanging around?" she said, hurrying to the small table beside her bed, unearthing the revolver from within.

"So, I'm going to shoot it and we're going to run back and get the girls. We'll get out of here and go read that poem. That will fix things, right?" Ray asked, gesturing for Laura to give him the gun.

"You want to read it together?" she asked, brain snagging on the implications as she handed over the weapon.

"Sure, I wouldn't let you do it alone. I..."

The sounds of something else sliding across the deck cut him off. There were a second and third body moving over the boards, others dragging their skin over the cement seawall, pressing through beach sand as they scaled the incline. From the noise, it was hard to pinpoint an exact number. It was safe to say many, all drawn to the final iteration of the poem, far more than the eight bullets in the revolver could handle.

"What do we do?" Ray asked, eyes traveling from one boarded window to the next.

"We wait. This happens every night. When the sun comes up, they usually just go away. They're kind of dumb, if I'm being honest."

"But what if they're not dumb this time? What if they get in?" Ray said, pointing to the only unobscured pane of glass, the seaweed-wrapped creature outside, pawing at the portal.

"Then we go back to your first plan and hope they can't run fast," Laura replied, retrieving the knife she'd stashed behind the television.

Ray nodded, moving to stand next to Laura before the window. The last gasps of sunlight sank into the sea, casting a final orange blear across the creature's waterlogged skin. Then the evening's shadows were all consuming, everything through the slim portal fading to grayscale. Laura could smell the sweat wicking off of Ray, could hear his heartbeat pulse in her ear. She was glad she wasn't alone on her last night in the cabin. She was glad at least one of her questions had been answered.

Together.

Not separate.

Now, all that was left was to find out what the poem would do to their world. If the words would tear some rent in the ocean floor and suck down all the sludge and smog, the pollutants and plastics and chemicals that never should have been... or would it vomit up more and more of the blind creatures who stalked about her home, scraping at the boards, hungry for what hid within.

Laura tightened her grip on the knife, leaning into Ray's side as they waited for morning to come.

It took three hours for the creatures to pull down the boards, leaving only bare glass between Laura and Ray and the gathered horde outside. The light from within made it hard to see much beyond their own reflections. Fangs bled through, and seaweed wrapped limbs, but there were so many bodies pressing against the cabin's walls, it was impossible to separate one silhouette from the next or see the ocean beyond. The single bullet and run plan was looking grimmer with each passing moment as the cabin's frame quaked under pressure. Then a window cracked in the eastern wall, a spider web of fractals creeping through the glass.

"I'm saying the skylight's our only way out," Laura said, pointing to the ceiling and the water stains ringing the aperture. "We've got to push the couch over."

"I thought you said waiting was the best option," Ray said, nervously chewing his lip, eyes darting from one exposed window to the next.

"I don't think there've ever been this many. We need to improvise or we're screwed," she said, bending to wrap an arm around the old sofa, pushing it across the hardwood. Ray bent to help as they aligned the furniture with the lowest point of the skylight. The ceilings weren't high, but they needed an added step if they were going to get out.

Laura stood on the back of the couch, Ray steadying her thigh with his free hand. She twisted the knob, opening the skylight to the chill night air. The mechanism was old and rusted and fought her at every turn as her home continued to shiver under the press of the creatures' mass. Eventually the skylight opened wide enough for their bodies to slip through, once Laura pushed the screen out of the way.

"When I'm out, hand me the pages," she said, pulling herself up.

Ray did as he was asked, pushing the gathered poem through the skylight once Laura steadied herself on the roof. Then he followed, revolver tucked into the waistband of his pants, metal cylinders clinking against one another, reminding them of the eight bullets, the eight chances they had to clear a path through the swarm.

Swarm was the only way to describe the gathering. Laura looked out over the sea of huddled bodies stretching down the beach as more and more emerged from the ocean. She looked over her shoulder to see if they were approaching Ray's house down the road, but most seemed to orbit her small cabin, never wandering far from her sun-like pull.

"There's no way...no way we're making it to the girls," Ray said.

"There's one way. Maybe. I'm still not sure, but I don't think we have another option," Laura said, sifting through the pages as she climbed to the cabin's peak, the moon's glow barely enough to make out the words written there. "We're close enough to the water and I can clearly see the ocean. The tide can carry these words to whatever ears it wants to."

Below, the creatures continued to dismantle the cabin, pulling shingles from the walls, dragging nails from boards, shattering glass. Laura didn't know how much longer the building could remain upright, how long before it pitched over and tossed them into the throng of grasping limbs and gnashing teeth.

"How long will it take you to read it?" Ray asked, hurriedly flipping on the light of his smartphone, aiming the beam over her shoulder so she could see.

"I don't think that matters anymore. This is either going to work or it isn't."

"Can't you just tell me it will? I need something to go on. Something—" Ray said, words seizing in his throat. His eyes turned to his home and the dim glow filtering through his front windows, his girls somewhere within, possibly unaware of what their father was facing, possibly hiding in fear for what lurked beyond their front porch. Laura didn't want the last thought she left Ray with to be one of despair, so she lied.

"Oh, it's totally going to work. A hundred percent. No doubt in my mind. Just hold that light steady and we'll be fine."

As Laura began to read, the creatures gathered below stopped pushing against the cabin, stepping back, tilting their heads towards the sound of her voice. It was as if the words were familiar, as if they were waiting for what came next. Laura didn't know what the final canto would bring, but their stasis gave her hope. The cabin wouldn't collapse after all. Maybe there was still a chance to be the healer her father sought. Maybe the oysters and the fish and the gulls and everyone else weren't doomed.

Laura flipped to the next page, the words unspooling from her tongue as if they'd always been waiting there, waiting for the right moment to slip free.

See Corey Farrenkopf's story "Translations for a Dead Sea" online at Metaphorosis.
If you liked it, leave a comment. Authors love that!
Remember to subscribe to our e-mail updates so you'll know when new stories are posted.

About the story

When I first moved back to Cape Cod after failing to find a teaching job after college, I worked for my uncle's fireplace company installing gas stoves. We did a lot of work on the Outer Cape, particularly in Ptown and Truro. The cabin this is based on is one of the dozens that you can see from the side of Route 6 when you head out towards the tip of the peninsula. We installed a few stoves in these over the time I worked there, usually freestanding propane units to take over for old, nonfunctioning woodburning hearths. These little shacks are kind of an odd, iconic segment of Cape Cod. They're tiny and sell for an ungodly amount of money and during moon tides are practically underwater. Picture a really waterlogged shed with a chimney. It seems like the owners are constantly fighting the sea, just dumping money into something they can't actually fight, which really matched up well with a climate change narrative. I wrote a number of stories set in and around these cabins, but nothing fit quite like "Translations for a Dead Sea". Being a person who is very obsessed with fixing problems and also being a person who has a ton of anxiety surrounding climate change, I always imagine what it would be like to figure out some way to make things better. If only I could find some forgotten Greek manuscript at an antique store, then we'd be all set. Remember, always keep your eyes out at flea markets and community swap meets. You never know what you'll find.

A question for the author

Q: How often do you think about writing during a day?

A: Until I've done it. Basically from the time I get up until the point I've gotten at least a handful of words down on the page, I'm thinking about what I should be writing. I usually get between 500 and 1,000 words done in a day, and once those are out of my head, I get a little euphoric bliss and can let myself play video games or something for a bit. Most weekdays I write during my lunch break, but often times its later in the day...and those days where I can't find the time at all, the words haunt me from sun up to sun down. Those are the worst days :)

About the author

Corey Farrenkopf is a writer of strange speculative fiction living on Cape Cod with his wife, Gabrielle, and their tiny dog, Ooli. He works as a librarian focused on spreading the good word of SF/F/H and Weird Fiction. He is also a member of the Blue Marble Librarians, which is a New England based group of librarians focused on climate change education and helping other libraries run environmental programs. He is also an active member of HWA.

@CoreyFarrenkopf

Copyright

Title information

Metaphorosis October 2023

ISSN: 2573-136X (online)
ISBN: 978-1-64076-267-1 (e-book)
ISBN: 978-1-64076-268-8 (paperback)

Copyright

www.metaphorosis.com

"Metaphorosis" is a registered trademark.

Discounts available

Substantial discounts are available for educational institutions, including writing workshops. Discounts are also available for quantity purchases. For details, contact Metaphorosis at metaphorosis.com/about

Metaphorosis Publishing

Metaphorosis offers beautifully written science fiction and fantasy. Our imprints include:

Metaphorosis Magazine
Plant Based Press
Verdage
Vestige

You can also find us:
Metaphorosis@writing.exchange
@Metaphorosis
www.facebook.com/metaphorosis

Help keep Metaphorosis running by supporting us at
Patreon.com/metaphorosis

See more about some of our books on the following pages.

Metaphorosis Magazine

Metaphorosis

Metaphorosis is an online speculative fiction magazine dedicated to quality writing. We publish an original story every week, along with author bios, interviews, and notes on story origins.

We also publish monthly print and e-book issues, as well as yearly Best of and Complete anthologies.

Come and see us online at magazine.Metaphorosis.com.

Plant Based Press

plant
based
press

Vegan-friendly science fiction and fantasy, including anthologies of the year's best SFF stories, from 2016-2020.

Chambers of the Heart

speculative stories
by
B. Morris Allen

A heart that's a building, a dog that's a program, a woman sinking irretrievably — stories about love, loss, and motion.

Susurrus

A darkly romantic story of magic, love, and suffering.

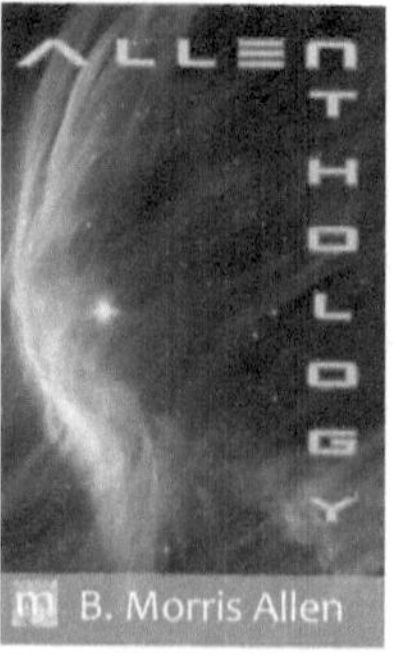

Allenthology: Volume I

Including three full collections of SFF stories.

Verdage

Science fiction and fantasy books for writers — full of great stories, often with an additional focus on the craft of speculative fiction writing.

Reading 5X5 x3

Changes

How do stories move from 'maybe' to published?

Here are 15 case studies of stories published in *Metaphorosis* magazine.

Reading 5X5 x2

Duets

How do authors' voices change when they collaborate?

A round-robin of five talented science fiction and fantasy authors collaborating with each other and writing solo.

Including stories by Evan Marcroft, David Gallay, J. Tynan Burke, L'Erin Ogle, and Douglas Anstruther.

Score

an SFF symphony

An anthology with an emotional score from the heights of joy to the depths of despair – but always with a little hope shining through.

Reading 5X5

Five stories, five times

See how different writers take on the same material.

Reading 5X5

Writers' Edition

Two extra stories, the story seed, and authors' notes on writing.

Vestige

Novelettes, novellas, and novels by Metaphorosis authors.

The Nocturnals
Mariah Montoya

Night is Dangerous. Day is deadly.

Where day and night last thirty years, humans move constantly stay ahead of the night and cruel Nocturnals that call it home. But a boy is lost out there.

Joyful Heave

Science fiction and fantasy anthologies with innovative and unusual themes.

Museum Piece
an unusual collection

A gallery of the strange and outrageous

Step right up and enter a world of wonder and oddities! These museums are not your typical tourist traps. From the Museum of Lost Dreams to the Suicide Museum, each exhibit will take you on a journey you won't soon forget.